W0007472

For Mum.
You taught me to love stories and history, and history's stories.

Prologue
Six Years Ago
"Life isn't fair."

Welcome to Tuesday, the 23rd of October; the day I'll kill my sister and start a war with the undead.

~

It's not fair, I say, pushing my face into the space between the front seats.

You'll get over it, says Dad. He leans further forward, his grip tightening against the steering wheel until his knuckles flush white. He grimaces as he peers into the writhing fog obscuring everything over six metres ahead of the car.

But, the pirate museum is open when we get there. Why can't we go? I say.

We've got all week to visit, he says.

I want to go tonight.

Well... you can't.

Why?

Because I'm your dad and my nerves are frayed and when we get to the cottage I'm going to... Jesus! He brakes hard, spinning the steering wheel to swerve around a sheep standing, eyes vacant, in the centre of the road. It *bahs* and fog rolls away from its lips. Dad inches the car forwards and in the rearview mirror I watch fog swallow the sheep.

That's settled it. When we get to the cottage I'm drinking a large, no... very large, glass of red wine. Possibly accompanied by Valium.

What's Valium? says Nugget, my younger sister, sitting alongside me in the back of the car.

Shut up Megan, I say. *I'm talking.*

Don't call me that, she snaps.

It's your name.

My name is Nugget!

She was right. We all call her Nugget, on account of her diminutive size and mop of iridescent golden hair, but I use Megan when I want to annoy her.

Will you be quiet! I'm trying to concentrate! shouts Dad. *We're not going to the museum today. End of.*

I can go on my own, I say.

You're ten, he says.

So?

So, no. Jesus, let it go, Tom.

I thump my head against the rear of his seat and whine. *It's not fair. It's the only thing I want to do on this stupid holiday.*

Well, consider it this stupid holiday's first life lesson: life isn't fair. He slows again as we turn a corner and mutters to himself. *Jesus, this is like a horror film.*

A life lesson, says Nugget jabbing a finger into my arm, nodding wisely.

You're weird, I say.

Mum! Tom said I'm weird.

Did he, says Mum frowning as she turns a map left and right trying to find a route to the village of Little Sickle. *That's... err... nice.*

Weird's not nice, says Nugget. She glances up at me, looking uncertain: *Is it?*

The locals call these fog banks a Sea Blind, says Dad. *They're the reason for all the wrecks around here.*

And we don't want to be another, so slow down, says Mum, looking up from the map.

I'm driving, you're navigating, says Dad.

You're driving too fast, Peter, slow down.

Here we go, I think. Here we go again.

Peter! Mum slams a hand against the dashboard. *You're not listening?*

Please don't argue again, please don't argue again, please don't argue again. Nugget is whispering her usual prayer. She curls against me like a puppy fearing the harsh words of its master.

I'm not driving too fast. I've been driving since I was sixteen. I was driving tractors when I was eighteen. Just concentrate on what you're supposed to be doing. If you'd paid attention at the last junction, we'd have been there half an hour ago.

Mum takes a deep breath, as if trying to calm her rising anger, then failing, spits out her frustration in a rush of words. *I told you to go left back at St Gideon. Don't. Blame. Me.*

Ha! You told me after we'd passed the turning. Navigation is pre-emptive, not reactive, says Dad.

You navigate then, she says stuffing the map into the space between his arms, chest and steering wheel.

You crazy cow! Are you trying to make us crash?

Pull over!

What?

I said, pull over!

He swerves over to the side of the road, tyres pop and grate over grit then judder over a cattle grid as we enter a field. Mum leaps out the car, tears running down her cheeks. Dad follows shouting.

Make them stop, says Nugget.

I ignore her, thinking: I hate them. I don't care what they say, I don't care what they do, I'm going to the museum tonight.

~

After they get back into the car, it only takes us another five minutes to find the sign announcing our arrival into Little Sickle, then we're pulling up at the cottage. The battle is over, but the cold war goes on.

Mum and Dad don't speak as they unpack cases and bags of food from the car.

Where's the sea? I say, turning and staring into the surrounding walls of fog.

Dad points away from the house, back down the drive.

What about the village?

He waves an arm indicating a left turn out of the drive. *Bring your stuff in*, he says.

I stand listening, fancying I can hear the distant boom of waves pounding cliffs.

I said, bring your stuff in. Dad drops my canvas backpack at my feet.

Nugget! I say snatching up the bag and inspecting the flowery felt tip designs now decorating its flap.

It looks pretty, she says.

I'm not a hippy.

What's a hippy?

In! Now! Shouts Dad.

Mum makes dinner; sliding spaghetti into one pan, pouring the ready made tomato sauce from a plastic tub into another. A cork pops free of a bottle and Dad heads in to the living room with his laptop, slurping from a glass.

I need to get an idea down, he says.

Mum doesn't reply.

Dinner passes with little more conversation than *please can you pass this or that* and then we are being packed off to the living room to occupy ourselves because Mum and Dad wanted to talk with a capital T.

Nausea swirls in my guts.

Are they getting a divorce, says Nugget? It's as if she could read my mind.

Who cares?

Oh, she says, then screws up her brow. *What is a divorce?*

I ignore her and walk out into the hall, a sudden certainty in the rightness of my actions powering my stride.

Where're you going? Nugget watches me wrestle my way into a jumper.

Before you ask, you're not coming, I say.

Why?

Because I said.

You sound like Dad.

No I don't.

I pull on my coat. Check the tenner is still in the pocket. Slip my arms into my backpack.

I'll scream, she says.

I sigh. *I'll pay you.*

She shakes her head. *I want to come.*

Growling, I throw her coat at her. The smile that lights up her face is almost bright enough to chase away my irritation.

~

I close the front door behind us, no more than a click of a latch betraying our departure. We turn left at the end of the drive and follow the road through the fog. What had Dad called it? A Sea Blind? The name made me think pirates. I imagine the weight of a cutlass in my hand and swish my arm through the fog setting it swirling.

There is no pavement and the grassy banks on both sides of the road, bordered by autumn-brown woods, are too slippery to walk on. So we walk along a road that is already matted with red, brown and gold leaves turning to mush.

Hold my hand, I say to Nugget, and she places her palm against mine, squeezing. Her hand feels smaller than usual, plump with warmth. She smiles up at me.

This is fun, isn't it, Tom, she says.

I nod even though all I feel is sadness. My sister could be the biggest pain in the world, seemingly incapable of retaining any information for over five minutes? *Why?* She'd ask. You'd answer. Later that day she'd hit you with the same *why?* She was a tell-tale and gossip. She drew flowery patterns with multi-coloured felt tip pens on my school books, bags, even on the back of my favourite Marvel t-shirt. And now she's scared. Scared of the black storm clouds that lash Mum and Dad with downpours of unreason and tears. She's scared, and I'm her big brother. Big brothers have responsibilities to little sisters. Mum and Dad made this very clear.

It's fun, I say, squeezing her hand.

The road descends, curving right and emerges from the trees to open spaces on both sides. A figure stands in the fog to our right.

Nugget dodges behind me, tugging my arm, pulling me into the road and whispers. *There's somebody there.*

I lean forward and peer into the gloom. *It's just a scarecrow. Come on,* I say, pulling her down the road.

He's watching us, she says glancing back over her shoulder once, twice, three times, until the scarecrow disappears from sight.

The white estate car comes out of nowhere. We've been concentrating on the scarecrow, lost in Nugget's imaginings and the fog has muffled the sound of its approach. Its horn blares, and wheels squeal, as it swerves. I yank Nugget from its path, clear into the air, dumping her onto the pavement, losing my balance and landing on top of her. Her heart lurches like an animal trying to escape a sack. The car speeds by, horn blaring and disappears into a swirling wall of white.

Naughty, says Nugget, as I help her to feet.

I'm lost for words, trying to catch my breath even though I have spent little energy. That had been so close. Close to Nugget. I clasp her hand in mine. Unfocused anger swells inside, pressing against my ribcage.

Never walk in the road again, I say, too loudly, too forcefully.

Her eyes fill with tears as she nods. *Do you think we should go back? They'll be worried.*

I shake my head. *We've come too far.*

And then, without pausing for any further thought, I set us on a collision course with the undead.

~

We pass stone cottages. Nearby, a church bell is ringing its peels stripped of their brightness by the fog. Then, the road is sloping down, steeply. I hear the sea and a surge of excitement washes against my black mood. The one thing that excites me about this stupid half-term trip - the single thing that will make it bearable - is the sea, or more accurately, the pirates that used it as their highway. Little Sickle had been a smuggling village, it had been a *pirate* village and now it had a pirate museum.

You're hurting my hand, says Nugget as I drag her along.

Sorry, I say. Then: *Come on, we're almost there.*

A road sign reads: The Bend. This is Little Sickle's main street, but even here the fog holds sway, rolling down the narrow space between cottages in ghostly coils.

Ha! I say pointing at a sign: Little Sickle Pirate Museum.

In a neighbouring street, a car's engine revs. Its tyres shriek against the road. It sounds like a sea monster in distress, calling out through the fog.

I expect the woman at the museum's ticket desk to question two kids going in alone at this time of day, but she takes my money, gives me a folded information leaflet, tells me the museum closes in thirty minutes and returns her attention to her magazine.

Pirates! I say to Nugget conjuring up a ghastly laugh.

My laughter doesn't last long; the museum is grubby and filled with nothing but aging display cabinets. It's dusty and dirty, the floor scuffed. Squares of cardboard are stuck over broken window panes. One has worked free and is rattling in a breeze.

Boring! sings Nugget.

I moved between the cabinets - many with broken locks meaning you could reach in and steal an exhibit, if you could find anything worth stealing - with increasing speed and growing frustration.

This sucks! There's one musket and a set of thumbscrews for torturing confessions from people, and a ship's log showing a page signed by the crew in faded, brown ink, but that is it. Where are the cutlasses and pistols, treasure chests and weather-beaten maps? Where are shark-teeth necklaces and hook hands – where's the fun?

Can we go now? says Nugget.

There are cabinets with diagrams of trade routes and pieces of paper stapled alongside them carrying long, boring explanations about... I don't know; it's all just too boring. Curling index cards, that have worked free of their staples, tell the stories of ordinary sailors forced into piracy by hard times, but make their lives sound dull. Where's the adventure? Where's the derring-do, the darkness of curses, black spots, Davy Jones Locker and making men walk the plank?

Pleasssssssse, says Nugget.

The most interesting exhibit is a cabinet housing a portrait of the Shark of the Straits, a pirate who had owned the big Manor House on the cliffs above the village. He stares out of the portrait with eyes dark as sea-wet rocks. Tattooed runes curl around his neck and across his hands. In his lap, he cradles a cutlass with a serrated blade as casually as a cup of tea. The serrations look like shark's teeth. A label by the picture says this is how he earned his name. Below the portrait is the Shark's wax death mask.

Nugget is tugging my hand.

We're at the end of the museum. *That was it*! Just one exhibit that stirred my desire for adventure and skulduggery. I feel robbed. Dad promised me a pirate museum and all I got was stuffy social history.

I have a whole seven days in this village and the one thing that might have helped fight off boredom has turned out to be a steaming pile of turd. I clench my fists. Open them. Place them on a cabinet. I want to smash something. I want to hear glass shatter, wood splinter. This has nothing to do with real pirates. My mind seethes. I'm so angry with Mum and Dad. I want them to come looking for us. I wanted them to care about us and stop tearing into each other. I want them to listen to me. I want...

Nugget? My hands are empty. I turn. She isn't there. Then I remember words heard, but not listened to: *I'm going back to the cottage.*

I hear the car scream; tyres and horn in unison.

I sprint through the museum and out the exit, fog twisting around me like exited ghosts. The white estate car that had nearly hit us earlier angles across the road. The driver's door opens and a big man with a beard staggers out. He looks at the front of the car and drops down onto his backside, oblivious to the puddle soaking his jeans.

Nugget!

A cottage door opens and a woman in a big, black cardigan steps out into the street. She screams and covers her face, her cardigan flapping like monstrous wings.

Nugget!

I half-walk, half-run across the road, fear tugging my movements like a drunken puppet master. I pass the driver. He appears unhurt, but his expression is vacant.

I didn't see her? He says. *She was like a ghost.*

When I step around the front of the car, I see blood.

Chapter 1
"The King of Little Sickle."

"There never used to be this many sets of traffic lights on the way into Little Sickle," says Dad, braking.

At the red light, a car with two adults in the front and three young teenagers in the back rolls to a halt alongside us.

"Ah, look at them, Peter, more fans," says Melloney, Dad's new younger wife, from the passenger seat. She's pointing at the kids.

"Cool," says Dad looking over his shoulder, a smile splitting his irritating, newly grown, hipster beard.

The kids are wearing pirate costumes. When they see Dad they explode into a fit of activity, pointing at him, clambering over each other to get to the window like puppies fighting over a bone. One of them opens the window and thrusts a copy of Dad's last book, *Return of the Demon Pirates*, towards the car. Two more copies join it, arms waggling in the air.

Even with my headphones on - listening to thumping Grime by Bentd Rizzle - and the car windows closed, I can hear them screeching for dad's autograph.

Dad reverses the car until he's level with them. His window buzzes open and their screeches invade the car. I turn down my music. I want to hear this. Nothing makes laugh more than hearing Dad suck up to his fans.

"By any chance are you going to the Little Sickle launch weekend for *King of the Pirate Demons*?" says Dad.

"Yes!" chorus the kids.

"Are you sure?" says Dad.

"Yes!" they roar.

Their mother lowers her window. "They're your biggest fans."

"And you three are my most favourite fans," says dad, scribbling his autograph in their books.

"You said that to the last lot," I say, too loud over my music.

"Ignore him," says Melloney, leaning across my dad to flash her perfect teeth at the mother. "Adolescent hormone blues."

"He's a teenager." The voice belongs to India, Melloney's nine year's old daughter by her previous husband. She's sitting next to me, sending deer-eared and doe-eyed pictures of herself to her friends on Snapchat. Even though the day is overcast, she's wearing big sunglasses beneath the sharp fringe of her black bob. India, AKA Indy, AKA the-most-irritating-step-sister-on-the-planet, no... in the universe.

The woman rolls her eyes. "I've got all that to come."

"It's such a shame," says Melloney.

The traffic lights change to green and cars behind us honk their horns. Dad waves to the kids as he pulls away. "See you in the Pirate's Nest!" He signs off with a corny pirate cackle. "Har har har!"

"Jeez," I say turning Bentd Rizzle up to ten and sliding lower in my seat. Then I see the sign for Little Sickle and it hits me. I try to control my breathing (*in through the nose, out through the mouth*) just like my counsellor told me too, but it doesn't help, it never does.

I'm falling back towards the dark days.

~

My memories of the months following Nugget's death are confusing, murky and unstable. There are holes, missing minutes, hours and even days, and sometimes I'm unsure what's a true memory and what's a memory of a nightmare. Does that count as a memory? I don't know. My counsellor says I may never recover all my memories. That's cool by me; there's nothing good back there.

I remember watching my parents lash out at each other, their marriage shattering under the mutual assault. I moved in with my mum, but a terrible guilt had her in its grip and it gorged itself on her. She lived on cigarettes and protein shakes. She withdrew from me, from herself, and finally from the world and had to be admitted to hospital. Her recovery would take a long time. She'd need medication. She might never be the same.

So I moved in with my dad. He welcomed me with open arms and with more forgiveness (*it wasn't your fault Tom, you must never, ever think that*) but I resented his resilience, his ability to carry on. I resented him letting me off because it *was* my fault.

Somehow, I moved forward, finding ways to cope. But it was like living in a world of snakes and ladders. Move the wrong number of emotional squares and... hey, where's the floor... I was plummeting down, backwards, snakes of guilt and anger swallowing me.

When he told me what he planned to do as his way of coping, I threatened to leave home, to run away and live rough. I couldn't understand how he could be so insensitive. How he could do this to Nugget's memory.

This is my way of preserving her memory, he'd said.

No, I said.

Yes, he said.

He wrote a children's book about a little girl named Golden and her adventures with a crew of supernatural pirates that set sail from a fictionalised version of Little Sickle. He'd been writing for years, trying to find fame and fortune without success. The death of his daughter finally brought this. The book, *The Demon Pirates*, was a bestseller. He sold the film rights and earned a five-book deal with a major publisher.

The Return of the Demon Pirates was the second book and this was an even bigger success. And now it was time to launch book three, *King of the Demon Pirates* at a weekend long event in Little Sickle culminating with a Grand Pirates' Ball on the Sunday.

My dad had returned to Little Sickle many times for research over the past six years. I'd never joined him, despite his urgings. I didn't want to come this time. I'd fought long and hard to avoid it, but I couldn't withstand a three-pronged assault from Dad, Melloney and Dad's agent, who thought my attendance would be good for Dad's 'brand'.

~

A glossy nail taps my knee. I turn my attention from the window to the space between the front seats. Melloney is staring at me, lips moving.

What? I mouth. *Can't hear.* I point at my headphones and shrug. Melloney raises an eyebrow threaded so severely it must be on an endangered species watch list. She says something else, maintaining her infuriating calm, and tucks a curl of auburn hair behind one ear.

My left headphone cup jerks away from my ear.

"She said: you should be excited for your dad," says India, shouting in my ear.

I prise her fingers from the headphones and smile. "I'm stoked," I say, replacing the cup and looking out the window.

We drive through the town, passing groups of kids in pirate costumes - my dad *har har haring* out the window at them - and then up to the hotel perched on the cliff edge above the village.

Melloney climbs out of the car. She's wearing Lycra leggings and a Lycra top. Pressing her palms together over her breastbone, she raises her arms skywards in back-arching semi-circles before returning her palms to the spot above her heart. She fills her lungs with a long breath and releases it. An exercise class called *Opportunistic Yoga for the Busy Modern Woman* is Melloney's current obsession. Every day, I find her stretching and bending while carrying out the most mundane of tasks: standing on one leg, hands pressed together while she waits for an egg to boil; standing on her head, legs against the wall while watching television. She catches me shaking my head, but ignores me. Instead, she turns to my dad.

"Peter, this place is absolutely darling," she says.

"It used to be a manor house belonging to the local landowner," he says looking at the ivy covered hotel. The sign standing proud of the green vines reads: THE PIRATES' NEST HOTEL & SPA. "Until he was kicked out by a pirate."

"The Shark at the Gates," she says.

"Of the Straits," he says, sounding annoyed at her slip.

"Yes, of course. I remember. Anyway, it's perfect."

Shielding his eyes, Dad stares out to sea. His brow furrows and he strokes the ridiculous beard he thinks makes him look younger. "I'm worried about the weather."

"It's not too bad. At least it isn't raining."

He pointed out to sea. "Look at the horizon. See that grey. Could be a Sea Blind coming in."

"A what?"

"A fog bank," I say, pleased to know something she doesn't.

"Well, that won't change anything, it'll just make things spooky," she says, making a *woo hoo* sound that I presume is meant to be a ghost.

Dad meets my gaze and I can see he's thinking what I am: *fog can change everything.*

He looks relieved to be whisked away by his agent. Some local journalists want to interview him. Melloney assumes the responsibility for getting the car unpacked and checking India and me into the hotel.

As I pull my suitcase from the boot, Melloney appears at my side.

"Why did you bring this old thing?" she says lifting my felt-tip decorated backpack with two fingers as if she might catch something from it. "If that's the only bag you have, I'll get you a new one in town."

I snatch it from her grasp. "You can't replace everything in my life."

"Now, Tom, that's not ..."

"Life's not fair, my dad taught me that," I say with a self satisfied smile and head for the hotel's entrance.

Chapter 2

"Be careful of the eyes."

India has a room connected to Dad's and Melloney's suite, but I have my own room.

"Jesus," I say entering the room. Fake pirate memorabilia decorate its walls: cutlasses and pirate clubs, artfully arranged sweeps of rigging and carved nick-knacks plundered from around the globe. My younger self, the self before I ever set foot in Little Sickle, would have burst with excitement at the thought of staying in such a room.

"We're having dinner, as a family, at eight," says Melloney, standing in my bedroom doorway. "It'll be the last chance for us to be together before the launch starts tomorrow."

"Key," I say, holding out my hand.

Melloney sighs, smiles. "For your dad's sake, can we try and get along this weekend?"

"You're not my mum."

"I'm not trying to be your mum."

"Then please may I have my key?" I say accompanied by a smile that could curdle milk.

She hands me the plastic rectangle decorated with the hotel's emblem, a scrimshaw tankard. Even on my short walk from the reception to my room I saw scrimshaw everywhere; tankards decorated with seafaring scenes on shelves, framed walrus tusks patterned with swirls, even the bedrooms' door handles are mock scrimshaw.

"Eight o'clock," she says.

"Counting down the minutes," I say, shutting the door.

I walk to my bedroom window. The sky has brightened, but the horizon is now a deeper grey. It seems to be closer. As if it took a giant stride towards us as soon as we turned our backs. *What time is it Mr Wolf?* Maybe Dad was right; there could be a Sea Blind on the way.

The thought calls a different fog into my mind. I'm lost in old memories. A maze without an exit. My heart races. My breathing is shallow. I need to take control.

In through the nose, out through the mouth.

In through the nose, out through the mouth.

How long I am gone for? When I refocus on the horizon, the room is cold and I know with absolute certainty that India is standing behind me. I hadn't heard the bedroom door open, but I'd really zoned out this time. This was India's great pleasure; sneaking up behind people and making them jump as she blurted out an obscure fact.

Did you know Costa Rica hasn't had an army since 1949?

Did you know the Romans sold fried mice as a snack in the coliseum?

And what frustrates her is that I can always catch her before she strikes.

'Ha!' I yell spinning to face her.

The room is empty and suddenly very cold. I blow into my hands and shudder. I was sure she was there. I could sense her, just like always. I open the wardrobe and check under the bed. I open the bedroom door and peer left and right down the corridor - nothing. I step back into the room and feel my body warming up.

I dial Melloney's room. She answers. "Peter Simpson's suite, can I help you?"

"Is India there?"

"Yes," she says.

"Can I speak to her? Please."

"Err... yes," she says suspiciously. I hear her call out to Indy.

India comes onto the line with her nine-year-old, wise beyond her years tones. "Hello Tom, how's your room?"

"Rectangular. Yours?"

"Same."

"Did you sneak into it?"

"Into what?"

"My room."

She snorts. "I'm under parental lockdown."

"Honestly. This is important."

In the background, a mobile phone plays a burst of music. Melloney answers the phone. India lowers her voice.

"I promise. Look, Mum has to help Peter with something soon and she's leaving me here on my own. She doesn't trust you to look after me. When she goes, I'm going exploring, want to come?"

She doesn't trust you to look after me.

I looked after another little girl once and...

"Are you listening to me?" says India.

"I've got stuff to do," I say and hang up.

What have I got to do? I don't even know what I'm doing here. I look out the window. The grey wall has crept forward again. I have a sudden urge to speak to my mum, to hear her voice, but something holds me back. I don't want to speak to her while I'm here. I don't want this place to seep back into her life. It's taken years for her to start getting better.

My phone beeps. A text message. It's my mum.

Are you okay??!!!

I stare at the message, feeling a tightness in my chest. My mum texts rather than calling. She's still fragile. She gets anxious on the phone. But to text now, just when I was thinking about her? That's freaky.

I'm fine. X

I had a nightmare. You were in it.

My heart sinks. This happens often.

Honestly I'm fine. ?

Please tell me you're not in Little Sickle!! ?

I consider lying, but she could text Dad to check and that would only make things worse. I curse him for not telling her. I shouldn't have to be the one. I need to keep this light.

Yep. Going to be a fun weekend. The town looks like the junior branch of Pirates of the Caribbean have taken over!! ??

I see three dots blinking. She's composing a response. It takes a minute before her next message pops onto the screen.

I can't believe he brought you back there! You have to promise me you'll be careful.

I promise. It's just a bunch of kids.

It was a bad nightmare.

I'm not sure if she means the past or her dream. She texts again before I can fire of a placatory reply.

It was about Scrimshaw.

Plenty of that here!! They should call this the Scrimshaw Inn ?

I saw scrimshaw eyes.

The room is getting cold again. There must be a gap around the window or something. I'll get Dad to speak to the front desk. I don't reply to Mum. I don't know what to say.

Scrimshaw eyes on you.

What the hell does she mean? I feel a panic rising inside me. I need to bring this conversation to an end. So I lie.

Got to go. Dad needs me for something. Love you. Take care. Xxxx

The three dots flash. I can't leave the conversation until she says goodbye.

I checked the weather. It says heavy fog is on the way. A Sea Blind.

It's just weather. I promise I'll be careful. Got to go. Xxxxxx

Ok. Bye. I love you. X

I get up and leave the room, feeling the need to at least act like I was telling the truth. As I descend the stairs towards the reception area, where I can hear an excited gaggle of junior pirates, my phone beeps again. It's Mum.

Be careful of the eyes.

I slip the phone into my pocket without replying, push my way through the crowd of kids and exit the hotel. I take deep breaths of salty air. Sea gulls wheel and screech overhead as I follow the curving road down to the village. I sense the grey horizon, now behind me, creeping ever closer.

My memories of the village are limited to that one terrible day, but even so I sense it's been transformed. I don't remember this many B&Bs, tea shops, restaurants and pubs, craft stores and pirate-themed gift shops. My dad's books have brought a mini tourism boom to the village which is why they were desperate to host this book launch weekend. My dad, the King of Little Sickle.

I drink an iced coffee in a cafe and Google the village. The first few pages of results are all linked to my dad's books. I dig through the Wikipedia entry to find something that isn't about Golden's adventures with the Demon Pirate and finally find something different. Alongside the tourists from all over the world brought by my dad's books, Little Sickle has witnessed a boom in ghost hunting. It now has the reputation as the most haunted village in Cornwall.

I follow an external link to the site of a man proclaiming himself to be the UK's *#1 Ghost Hunter Extraordinaire*. He has a page dedicated to a recent visit to Little Sickle. It includes a gallery of grainy photographs claiming to show ghosts he captured with his state of the art equipment. I click through the gallery.

Image 1: unknown figure in St John's graveyard. (This is wishful thinking; a shadow beneath a tree with tombstones in the background.)

Image 2: pirate #1 in cellar of Two Cutlasses public house. (Come on! That's just a trick of the light. If he hadn't suggested it was a figure, you would never have guessed.)

I consider clicking away but look at one more picture to confirm my righteous scepticism.

Image 3: Unknown girl on The Bend.

I click away from the link. A shiver runs through me and I blow into cupped hands. Why did I order an iced coffee when I feel so cold all the time? That's just stupid.

I leave the cafe and head back to the hotel feeling even more depressed than when I left. As I reach the doors, I see tongues of fog licking the cliff edge. The Sea Blind is here. I hurry inside.

I'm just putting my key into my door when I sense India behind me. Please be there. I spin around.

"How do you do that?" She grimaces with annoyance. For reasons best known to her, she's still wearing her sunglasses.

"What's that?" I point at the cardboard box - the shape and size of a family pizza box - in her hand.

"A Ouija board."

"Yeah, right," I say.

"It is."

"Melloney let you bring a Ouija board?"

"No, silly. I found it in the hotel's attic."

This was typical India; information woven into a fantastic tale. Digging the truth out of her was like story archaeology.

"You just happened to go exploring the attic and found a Ouija board."

She removes her sunglasses. "Doh, no! The girl told me it was up there."

"What girl?"

"I don't know her name."

"So, an unknown girl tells you to look in the hotel's attic, you do, and you find a Ouija board? Am I getting this right?"

"Yes."

"Where did you meet her?"

"I didn't meet her, I heard her."

I consider shutting my bedroom door on this nonsense, but what else do I have to do in this stupid village.

"How come the invisible girl talked to you."

India shrugs. "Young minds are more open, maybe."

"What else did this girl say?"

"That she needs to speak to you," she says, lifting the Ouija board. "Through this."

Anger flares in me. She's playing a dangerous game here. Straying into areas she shouldn't. She may be young but that was no excuse. I turn to my door.

"You should talk to her," she says.

"Oh, yes. Why?"

"You might like her. You need a girlfriend."

"No I don't "

"You should have one at your age."

I give her a sour smile. "So says the nine year old agony aunt."

"Agony sister," she says.

I lean forward. "You're not my sister."

I realise too late how hard the words have come out. She turns away, eyes filming with tears and slides her sunglasses back on.

"Whatever," she says, retreating to her bedroom door.

I open my mouth to call to her, to apologise, but I'm too slow. Her door clicks closed. I spin around, sensing somebody behind me again, but find an empty corridor. I hate this place. I hurry into my room.

It's cold inside and there's condensation on the window. In the middle of the pane somebody has written one word: Ouija. A dribble of water runs down the pane from the bottom of the letter i. I stand still, staring at the word. Goosebumps rise across my flesh.

How?

I cross the room and scrub away the word with a palm. India must have done this. She stole a spare key from my dad, sneaked in and wrote this just before I returned; that was how.

I sense somebody behind me again, but this time I don't turn around. I stare out the window willing them to go away. Outside the world is grey with fog.

Chapter 3
"They're breaking through."

Our family dinner is a strained affair. Dad does his best to lighten the mood with jokes, but it doesn't work. I can see he's relieved to have the constant distraction of village dignitaries, and teenage fans, passing the table and telling him how much they adore his books and just cannot wait to read the new one.

India, for once minus sunglasses, is uncommonly quiet. Melloney keeps glancing at her and then skewering me with an accusatory stare. I wonder if India told her about my *you're not my sister* comment.

The village's mayor strides up to the table. He's a very tall man, stooped as tall people often are, and sports a waxed moustache finished with dashing, upward twists. "Ha ha, the Royal Family at dinner," he says slapping my dad on the shoulder.

"Mayor Urquhart, how are you?" says Dad, pushing back his chair and standing.

"Oh, please don't let me interrupt," says the Major.

"It's no problem," says Dad.

Melloney raises one of her endangered-species eyebrows and fixes Dad with a please-don't-leave-me-alone-with-these-two stare.

"Well... if you're sure. I'd like to introduce you to Councillor Timms," says the mayor.

"Of course... of course," says Dad and they make their way across the dining room, stopping at most tables to shake hands.

"I've got an earache," says India. She presses a hand against her left ear. I'm expecting her to follow this up with a joke about how I caused it, but she looks genuinely distressed.

Melloney leans close. "How long have you had it for, darling?"

India shrugs. "Half an hour. It really hurts. And it sounds all funny. Like I can hear echoing voices."

"Do you want me to get painkillers?" I say.

Melloney stares at me. "Feeling guilty. About your *sister*," she says.

My face colours, violently, fuelled by a mixture of embarrassment and anger. I know Melloney is attacking me for my harsh words to India, but doesn't she realise what she'd just said. Where we are? What had happened to my *real* sister here?

I push back my chair and it falls, clattering against the wooden floor. A sudden, pained realisation pinches Melloney's face. "I didn't mean *that*," she whispers. "Sit down. Please, Tom."

I can see my dad looking at me across the room, a look of horror ill concealed beneath his hastily erected, and wholly false, smile. His eyes plead with me to sit down and shut up. But he's not alone. I feel the eyes of the room spear me from a hundred perspectives; the weight of their knowledge and the force of their judgement.

The words erupt from me. "That's right, I'm the boy who killed Golden!"

I storm out of the restaurant, into the lobby and out into the night. Dense fog embraces me in its clammy tendrils. It's taken over the night. There's no moon, no stars, no sea, no trees, just fog.

"Tom, what the hell's going on?" It's Dad, emerging from the hotel.

I turn to face him as Melloney follows him into the night.

"Peter, this is my fault. I was worried about India; I wasn't thinking what I was saying. I said something that was easy to take the wrong way." She walks past Dad and stands close. "I'm sorry, Tom. Really, I am."

"No, this is my fault," says Dad. "It was stupid and selfish of me to bring him. I had this voice whispering in my head saying it was a good idea, but in my heart I knew he wasn't ready."

I take a step back into the fog. I can't control my feelings now. They're like a severed electrical cable, sparking, thrashing. "Stop being so bloody understanding. It was my fault. Mine! I did it and I can never, ever take that back."

I don't see Dad move, but his arms are around me. I'm crying. I never cry. Crying doesn't help. It's temporary. The pain's still there when you stop.

"Let me go!" I shout, thrashing against him, but he doesn't.

The electricity of my rage spends itself and suddenly I'm empty. I let Dad lead me back into the hotel, up the stairs, into my bedroom. He helps me to get undressed. I climb into bed.

"I'm sending you home tomorrow. There's a train from Fetchcliff-on-Sea. I'll call your auntry Jess; she'll look after you.

Even in my current numb state, it's a relief that this ordeal is over. I swear to myself that I'm never coming back to Little Sickle.

~

Sleep snatches me, but it isn't restful. My dreams are thick with the Sea Blind. The hotel's walls and doors have become fog. The ceiling roils above me. Fog forms a quilt as heavy and cold as stone. It crushes my chest. I can't breathe. Can't move. Can't escape its crippling embrace. The bedroom door flows open and a figure enters. Fear galvanises me to greater action. I try to wrestle free of the bed. I can't. The figure approaches me. It's man-shaped fog; the Sea Blind made flesh.

It presses its thumbs against my eyes and I'm in darkness. It's saying something, the words wheezed out, only an echo of a whisper. The pressure on my eyes increases. The thumbs are hot as a fire's embers. My arms are held fast. I take deep breaths, trying to summon energy, and I smell the figure. It isn't made of fog alone; there's fog and smoke twisting together.

I sense the figure bending closer as it increases the pressure, driving downwards through its thumbs. A scream forms in my chest, but as I draw a breath to fling it out, my mouth fills with smoke. I hear one word amidst the whispering - *scrimshaw* - then the figure leans all its weight onto its thumbs and my eyeballs pop.

I wake, wrestling against the weight of my quilt, heart lurching, lungs pumping as if I had run a cross-country race. Propping myself on an elbow, blinking, I scan the room. It's empty. The bedside clock reads: 03:15. I grab the little bottle of water on the bedside table and guzzle it down. As I finish it, catching my breath, footsteps pad up to my bedroom door. Floorboards creak beneath each step, then stop. I hold my breath. The creaking footsteps continue down the corridor.

I pinch myself. Is this a dream within a dream? I get up, pull on jeans and a t-shirt, open my bedroom door and peer out. The corridor is lit by the subterranean-green glow of emergency exit signs at each end, but it's empty.

I step out, seeing Dad's bedroom door ajar. I hesitate. Peering in, all I see is darkness. What's going on here? I push the door further open, waiting for the hinges to betray me with a squeak, and when they don't, I slide inside. The glow of the bedside clock illuminates the rising and falling shapes of two figures spooning in bed; Dad and Melloney.

Dad coughs and turns over. Melloney mutters something. I stand still, holding my breath. When they settle down, I creep another three metres into the room. Now I can to peer through the door that opens onto India's room. Her bed is empty. The duvet tossed back. There's no sign of her elsewhere in the room. I back out into the corridor.

My bedroom door is open wide. I didn't leave it like that. I tiptoe inside. India is standing in the middle of the room. She's wearing her favourite skull-patterned pyjamas. Her arms hang loose as string at her sides. Her eyes are open but unfocused.

"India?" I say.

She remains still and unresponsive.

I take a step closer. "India, you're sleepwalking. Wake up."

She doesn't move. Dare I shake her awake? I think you're supposed to avoid doing that with sleepwalkers, it can be dangerous. I had a friend at school called Jason Duvall, he was a chronic sleepwalker. He'd wander into his parents' room, downstairs and even out into the back garden. One night his dad tried to wake him and Jason sprinted around the garden convinced he was being chased by a woolly mammoth. He broke three toes when he kicked a paving slab.

One last time, I try waking India with words. "India, it's me, Tom. Wake up, your sleeping."

There's no response. I step forward to shake her.

"They're breaking through," she says, just as I'm about to touch her.

I pull my hands away. There's something wrong with her voice. It's flat, lifeless. It doesn't sound like her.

"India, wake up."

"They're breaking through."

The room is cold again. I shiver. Maybe if I played along with her, I could lead her out of the dream.

"Who's breaking through?" I say.

"The deathlings."

I've never heard the word before, but it chills me. I'm thrown. I don't know what question to ask next. Her voice is changing again. This is wrong. I'm getting goosebumps on goosebumps.

"You woke him. Now you're back. He's stronger. All he needs is what you have. Then he can bring them all with him."

"Who's he?" I say.

Her voice has lost its lifelessness and taken on the animated tones of a girl. A young girl.

"The Shark."

"Stop it, India. This isn't funny."

"He wants his eyes, Tom. You can't let him have them," says India, in Nugget's voice.

"Stop it," I say.

"I have to go now. This is too hard. And if I stay any longer, I'll hurt India. Use the Ouija board, please Tom. I have to explain everything."

"Stop it," I shout this time, shaking India by her shoulders.

Her face has collapsed into a vacant expression again. A true sleep-walker's face. Her arms flap at her sides. Then she moans, it's a terrible sound born out of terror. Violently, her face is changing, as if a carved mask has been pushed to the surface stretching her skin, distorting it.

A scream rips out of India. "Get it out of my head!" I stumbled backwards hitting the wall as incoherent wails pour out of her. "Get out, get out, get out! Bad person!"

Feet thunder into the hall and Dad and Melloney, both dressed in t-shirts and pants, run into the room. Melloney dashes to India. Her face has returned to normal. Now she's panting, eyes open, struggling for focus.

"Darling, what happened? Are you okay? Speak to me? Please," says Melloney.

Dad stares at me.

"She was sleepwalking," I say. "I tried to wake her by speaking to her but..." I shrug.

He puts a hand on my shoulder as understanding as ever. Why isn't he ever angry?

"Bad person in my dream," says India. "A pirate."

"No more reading Peter's books for you then." Melloney wipes tears from her daughter's cheeks.

"Hey," says Dad, a crestfallen look on his face.

"Not now, Peter," says Melloney, following her words with a we'll-talk-about-this-later expression.

"Of course," says Dad.

Melloney glances at me but doesn't speak as she lifts India into her arms and carries her out of the room.

"Night, son," says Dad, then gives me his saddest look. "I'll get you on that train first thing. You going to be okay on your own until then?"

I nod.

"Good lad," he says as he closes the door.

But I'm not alone, I know that now. Nugget's here. And she needs my help. As much as I hate Little Sickle, I can't leave it now.

Chapter 4

"Cat got your tongue?"

The next morning, I stand outside Dad's bedroom door. I take a deep breath. I can't let him send me back to Manchester now. Nugget is here - as mad as that sounds to me in daylight - she's here and she needs my help. I need India's Ouija board to talk to her again. I knock on the suite's door. Dad opens it, looking down at his smart phone.

"I don't want to go home. I want to stay. And help. I promise to stay out of trouble. I'll babysit India, I'll help set up the ball, I'll paint the hotel. I'll do whatever you say. Just don't send me home." The words tumble out of my mouth

He looks up at me. Opens his mouth to speak.

"Please. Give me another chance," I say.

He holds up the phone to show me a railway app display; all the trains from Fetchcliff-on-Sea are cancelled.

"You'd think they could build trains tough enough to smash through fog, wouldn't you?" He says shaking his head. "I'm not happy about this. I made a mistake bringing you here."

"I'm okay, Dad. Honestly."

"No you're not."

"I am."

He looks at me. "You sure?"

"Yes."

"It's just a couple of days," he says, as if he's trying to convince himself, not me. "We'll get through this together, okay?"

"Okay," I say, trying not to show just how relieved I am by this turn of events. I look past him into the room. The image of the face pushing up through India's flashes in my mind. I blink the memory away, but my skin crawls. "How's India?"

"You know what's she like, little Miss Rubber Ball. She bounces straight back."

"Can I speak to her?"

"She out with Melloney running errands. They're sorting out last minute details for the ball."

"When will they be back? I want to make sure she's okay."

"She's fine, I told you." He squints at me. "Where's this sudden concern for India's welfare come from?"

My thoughts spin. I don't want to raise his suspicions. I need to calm down. Pick my moment to speak to her.

"I said something really mean to her the other night. I want to make things right." I give him my best hangdog, sincere expression.

"I appreciate that son," he says placing a hand on my shoulder and squeezing. "She thinks of you as her big brother. You can speak to her this evening when she gets back."

This evening!

"In the meantime, you and I can have some man-time. We're going to help set up the dining room for tonight's surprise event." His face lights up. "Want to know what it is?"

The format for this weekend's book launch has been in place for months, but Saturday night's entertainment has been kept a secret, even from me and India. Friday is the informal arrival dinner. Sunday is the official book launch, with a reading by Dad, followed by the fancy dress Grand Pirates' Ball which was open to the entire village and the army of his fans that had arrived from around the globe. Saturday evening is billed as *A Thrilling Surprise Event*.

"Hit me," I say.

He mimes a drum roll. "It's only the world-premiere, sneak preview, of the film of *The Demon Pirates*!" He jumps up in the air, landing with arms and legs spread wide.

I'm impressed. "Really?"

"Really." He claps his hands and I smile at his childish excitement. "Cool, eh? The cast are arriving later today if they can find their way through the Sea Blind. Come on, there's lots to do," he says closing the door and leading me down the hall.

~

For the rest of the morning Dad and I help the events team convert the hotel's ballroom into a cinema. I have never seen him so excited.

We erect staging to ensure everybody has a good view of the huge screen now filling the wall at the far end of the room. Speakers rise like Stonehenge monoliths. Stacks of chairs wobble on trolleys as we wheel them in. We build a popcorn stand and then bar to serve pirate-themed drinks. Rigging, nets and several Jolly Rodgers are hoisted high as decoration. Dad says they'll be left in place for the ball.

We eat a lunch of sandwiches and fruit with the events crew who are a fun bunch. They're all in their early twenties and sport multiple tattoos, sagging jeans, long hair and hipster beards. They throw questions at my dad asking about the film; Hollywood's purchase of his books has elevated his celebrity status to a new level. Eyes bright, they listen to his tales of meeting hard-nosed producers and how he sat in on casting calls full of starlets.

"Cool beard, Mr Simpson," says one of the crew to my dad, as he pulls his phone from his pocket to check a message. "Do you wax it?"

Dad strokes his beard, nearly exploding with delight. "Errr... no, should I?"

"Yeah. Give me your number, I'll text you a couple of good brands," says the youth, stroking his own beard.

"Cool," says Dad. Surely, this day couldn't get any better for him.

When we finish eating, the crew head out to the van to collect more props leaving us alone. "I've got press interviews in the bar now. You can come and sit in, or you can stay and help here. If you promise to stay out of trouble," he says giving me a playful punch on the shoulder.

"I'll stay here," I say.

"Okay. Laters," he says striding off. If I'm not mistaken, he's loosened his belt so that his jeans sag down at the back. I shake my head. It won't surprise me if he has tattoos when I see him later.

As soon as he leaves the room, I head for reception.

"Can I have the key for my dad's room please? I need to get papers for his interviews."

There's no hesitation from the man behind the desk - I am part of the Royal Family.

"Thank you," I say, heading for the stairs.

I search India's room with no success and then move onto Dad's; still nothing. Where's she hidden the Ouija board? I go back over both rooms with the same result and stomp downstairs.

The hotel's Library, a lounge where they serve afternoon tea, is the only room not taken up with party planning and so I slip inside planning to wait for India to return. It's a grand room with crammed bookcases lining one wall. Opposite this are tall windows that should offer a view of the lawns, cliffs and ocean, but the fog presses close against the leaded panes obscuring the world. There's a log fire cracking in the hearth, but the room seems unnaturally cold. I turn, sensing somebody behind me. There's nobody there, but a portrait of the Shark of the Straits stares down at me from the wall. I remember this picture. There was a copy of it in the pirates' museum.

My conversation with India/Nugget pops into my mind.

Who's he?

The Shark.

He wants his eyes, Tom. You can't let him have them.

In the painting, The Shark is sitting in a chair staring out at the observer. There's no escaping his dark gaze; wherever you stand in the room, he's staring at you. He wears a jacket of rich purple satin and beneath this a white shirt with a frilly collar and cuffs. His genteel dress contrasts with the tattooed runes and symbols ringing his throat and twisting around his fingers. A serrated sword rests casually in his right hand, its white scrimshaw handle, decorated with a dragon's head.

I take a step forward. "What do you want from me?"

The Shark doesn't answer, but somebody else speaks.

"It's rude to ignore people." The voice is female with a rich West Country accent.

I spin around. The girl is standing by the fire, looking at me with bright green eyes that twinkle with amusement. She has long, curly black hair tied into a ponytail with a piece of rope as thick as a finger, high cheekbones and a pale, almost sallow, complexion. Maybe she spends too long in dark rooms watching her boyfriend's band rehearse. Where did that thought come from? Why am I even thinking about her having a boyfriend?

She's wearing a white shirt much like the Sharks, but tighter, and a pair of leather trouser that end mid calf. A tattooed snake curls around her right calf. She's barefoot. How old is she? Fifteen, sixteen or seventeen; it's difficult to tell. I blush beneath her gaze.

"Cat got your tongue?" she says.

"I think you're a bit early for the Grand Pirates' Ball," I say, pleased to have dug out a nugget of wit

"Funny, ha ha," she says, smiling. "Waiting staff have a dress rehearsal this afternoon. The powers that be want to make sure us locals know how to treat our betters." She curtsies to me.

For some reason, this girl has me tongue tied. Well, that's a lie, there's an obvious reason for my tongue-tiedness: she's exceptionally hot. I wrestle a question from my mouth.

"What's your name?"

"Eloise. Your Tom Simpson, son of the famous Peter Simpson, saviour of Little Sickle." It was a statement tinged with sarcasm, not a question.

"Guilty," I say.

"Are you?"

"Definitely."

"What's the sentence for your guilt?" She walks across the room to stand two metres in front of me. She smells of the fire.

"To be known as my father's son."

"Hmmm." She steps past me and points at the portrait of the Shark. "Do you know what happened to him?"

I shake my head. "I read something in the museum, but that was a long time ago. Didn't he die at sea?"

"Ha, that stuff in the museum is all lies. The village doesn't like to talk about the truth."

"What do you mean?"

"They killed him. Burnt him and his crew alive."

"Who, the villagers?"

She takes a step closer to the painting. "They didn't like having him as their lord and master. Thought his ways were rough and uncouth, even though he brought prosperity to the village. They enjoyed the money, you see, and fancied becoming a town of substance. So they betrayed him. They raised a false alarm, told him the army had come down from London looking for pirates. Him and his crew headed out to their ship - The Dragon Maiden - but the villagers had been there before, hidden by a Sea Blind, filling the hull with barrels of oil. Soaking the deck too. When the Shark and his crew were aboard, the villagers set it ablaze. All it took was a flaming arrow fired from a row boat. They all burnt alive, except for his daughter. The Shark threw her overboard."

"She survived?"

The girl shakes her head and speaks in a sing-song voice:

"*She struck her skull,*
Upon the hull,

And fell unto the sea,
Oh glory be,
How this day was crowned,
As the Devil's daughter drowned."

"A pretty rhyme made up by the god-fearing villagers to celebrate a young woman's death. There were others too, but few remember them now."

"How do you know all this?"

She ignores me. "Have you noticed that throughout history, when ordinary people, the *normal* people, do ugly things they are forgotten or forgiven?

"Look, I didn't know any of this."

"And we won't hear any of these facts mentioned in your father's interviews this weekend, will we?" She looks over her shoulder at me. "Our village history has been re-written. Made fit for children."

"He didn't rewrite the history. He's not a historian, he writes kids' books," I say moved to defend Dad. "Anyway, how do you know so much about what happened?"

"You think I'm lying." She turns around. Her eyes aren't twinkling anymore.

"I didn't say that."

"What did you say then?"

"It's just that if you know so much, you might be able to help me."

"My father has studied this village for a long time. He's a historian, of sorts. How can I help you?"

I lick my lips, unsure whether to go on.

"Out with it," she says. She moves forward. She's standing too close. I see myself reflected her eyes.

"Have you heard of the Shark's eyes? Something, an object maybe, he called that, or..." My words dribble away to nothing. "Sounds bonkers doesn't it?"

"What are you on about?" She shakes her head and smiles draining away the tension.

"I know; I don't even understand what I'm asking. Forget it."

She pulls her ponytail over her shoulder and toys with it. I can't look away from her gaze.

"I can show you a secret that's linked to the Shark. Maybe it'll help, maybe it won't. But it'll be fun." She moves away from me and stands in front of a bookcase. She counts down three shelves, removes two books and reaches into the resulting space. There's a clunking sound and one side of the bookcase swings into the wall on squeaking hinges revealing a shadowed passage beyond. She steps inside.

"Coming?" She says. "Or are you chicken?"

Chapter 5
"Do you still think me pretty?"

I follow Eloise through the bookcase door. She reaches past me, her face nearly touching mine, and swings the door closed, plunging the passageway into darkness. My skin tingles in response to her proximity. She laughs and makes a comedy *woo-hoo* ghost noise. I tug my smartphone from my pocket and flick the torch app into life.

"Don't shine that in my eyes," she says blinking.

"Sorry." I turn the light down to its lowest setting. It gives Eloise's face an unhealthy green sheen, as if she'd drowned and risen from the sea. I guess I look just as ghostly to her.

I play the light around the corridor. It's a tight space, wood-panelled and filled with great arcs of spiders' web that wouldn't have looked out of place in the cheesiest of horror films.

"Scared yet?" she says.

"Petrified."

She laughs and, with a nod of her head, sets off down the corridor. She sweeps her arms through the air clearing cobwebs, ducking her head to avoid the most prodigious. I follow, trying to shine the light past her to illuminate the way, but only highlight her shapely bum moving purposefully beneath the taut material of her trousers.

"What did they use this tunnel for," I say, trying to distract myself from her body's rhythmic motion.

"Spying on guests; there are passages linking most on the rooms on the ground floor and others upstairs. And for escape."

The passageway splits, one branch runs straight ahead, the other is a wooden staircase descending into darkness. She increases her pace as she takes the stairs.

"This must be below the level of the house," I say.

"Clever, aren't you," she replies and disappears into shadow.

"Hey, wait."

The wooden stairs rattle and creak beneath our steps. The air is getting cooler. Eloise giggles as she darts into another turn, another set of stairs descending into darkness.

"Keep up," she says.

"Where're you taking me?" I say, trying to keep my voice level.

She glances back. "Looking for answers."

The passage slopes downwards. Now the walls are slick, bare stone and the floor is sandy. The ceiling is high and lost in shadow. I can feel the sea pounding the cliffs through my soles. There are more turns, more side passages.

"This is like a maze," I say.

"It is a maze, a pirate's maze, designed to confuse customs men and soldiers," she says. "And you."

She comes to a halt and turns to face me. "Here we are?"

I move the torch beam around the walls. "I don't see anything?"

"Do you know where you are?" She says. "Could you find your way back on your own?"

"Probably not," I lie. There's something wrong about this.

"Then we've arrived at our destination: the place where you are lost."

"What are you talking about? If there's nothing to show me, let's go back. Now."

She sighs. "There's much to tell you. And to show you. But you need to remember things first." She takes a step towards me.

I step away. "Look, I get it. You resent my dad writing kids' books about pirates and your village because it belittles the truth of what really happened. Honestly, I get it, and I sympathise with you, but what do you expect me to do?"

Too quickly for me to avoid, she reaches out and clicks the forefinger and thumb of her right hand in front of my forehead. I glimpse tattoos at the base of both digits, but I can't see what they are.

I stagger on the spot. I'm blind. My vision a black canvas on which images flicker.

I'm in Little Sickles' pirate museum. I'm ten years old. Nugget, bored and twisting her golden locks around one finger, stands next to me. I look into a display case. It contains a locket that belonged to the Shark of the Straits. The locket is open to display a small painting within. It's a painting of a pretty girl with long, dark curly hair and green eyes. The label alongside the locket says: Eloise Francis, daughter of the pirate Bartholomew Francis, also known as The Shark of the Straits.

Then, I'm back in the passage. My head hums. The sea pounds against the cliffs, its violence rising through my body. I place a hand against the wall, steadying myself, and stare at Eloise. She nods and starts off in her sing song voice, only this time, when she speaks, sea water gushes from her mouth filling the corridor with its salty smell.

"*She struck her skull,*
    Upon the hull,
    And fell unto the sea,
    Oh glory be,
    How this day was crowned,
    As the Devil's daughter drowned."

"You can't be," I say.

"Oh, but I am. The Devil's daughter. And I'm here to tell you how to bring my father back to me." With every word, sea water spews from her lips, soaking her chin and shirt, but not a drop reaches the ground.

"No, this isn't real. How can I see you if you're dead?"

"Because you own something of power. And because I wanted you to see me."

I edge way from her, every muscle twitching to take flight. But if I run that means I've accepted what I'm seeing. "I don't believe in ghosts," I say, and the words sound feeble.

"And you are right not to," says Eloise. "There are no ghosts, just the living, the dead, and those in between; the deathlings. Deathlings are the dead who haven't yet passed on because they're scared of the light, or because they're pulled back to the land of the living by unfinished business. I'm a deathling." She coughs and splutters, then, bending forward, pulls a long, frilly edged blade of seaweed from between her lips.

It's enough for me to believe. I twist around, sprinting, any thought of trying to retrace our previous route - that I *had* memorised - lost in my blind panic. I'm sure her fingers will close around my shoulder at any second, but they don't. Maybe I've outrun her. I skid to a halt, panting, then hold my breath, listening for the sound of pursuit. The tunnel is silent. I jog forward, turn a corner.

Eloise blocks the tunnel. A small crab clambers from one of her nostrils.

"You must listen to my story, Tom," she says.

"No." I shake my head but she continues talking.

"My father lived a dangerous life and had many enemies. To protect himself, he had his body tattooed with magic runes in the lands of the Orient. These runes protected his soul. Men knew if they betrayed him, his soul would return to take vengeance on them."

I'm talking over her, refusing to listen. "Leave me alone, please, I haven't done anything to you, or him." I try to back away, but stumble, landing on my arse on the sandy floor. "Eloise, please, I begging you."

"*Eloise, Eloise*, yes, once I was Eloise, the pretty pirate princess." An anguished expression crosses her face, then somehow she is centimetres from me. She is biting the inside of her mouth. I think there are tears in her eyes. "You thought me pretty when I stood by the fire. I could see the desire in your eyes. Do you still think me pretty?"

Salt water falls from her mouth, vanishing before it touches me. Her lips are slick with it. A sliver of seaweed dangles from her chin. The little crab scuttles across her cheek and disappears into her right ear. I remember the painting in the locket. The girl standing by the fireplace in the library. The smell of fire on her skin.

I force out the word. "Yes.

Her eyes hold mine. A tear falls, running down her cheek. It's made of blood. She brushes it away, smearing it across her pale flesh.

"It's of no consequence," she says and stabs a finger towards me. "Now listen well, Tom Simpson. Listen and mark what you must do."

"The villagers of Little Sickle learned of my father's tattoos, knew they must have magic to fight magic. So, they pooled their wealth and sent a merchant to the secret markets held in the shadows of London's docks. There, the merchant purchased two magical, scrimshaw coins, carved from the bones of a whale that only swims through oceans in our dreams."

"These coins were crafted by a magician in the court of the Sultan of Zanzibar. The magicians name was Ullman ul Haq and he made many magic objects; a trinity of daggers that would always return to their master, playing cards with hidden suits that could open doors to other worlds, a flute that could summon deathlings."

"But it was the scrimshaw coins the villagers needed. Coins carved with the energy that exists at the point where life meets death. Place them on the eyes of a dead man and his soul would be locked inside the coins for all time. The only way to release him would be to break the coins in the very building where they were placed upon his eyes."

I drag myself away from her. Arms spread wide. Palms pressed to each wall as I haul myself upright. I cannot follow the madness of what she is saying; magicians and scrimshaw eyes, souls locked away, the point where life and death meets. Surely, I'm going to wake up at any moment.

"This is no dream," says Eloise, as if she can read my mind.

"What does any of this have to do with me," I shout, finding reserves of strength to channel into anger.

"You have the coins," she says.

I shake my head, incredulous. "I don't have them. I've never heard of them. I don't know what you're talking about."

She's standing in front of me and then she isn't. I spin around again. She's centimetres from me. Before I react she clicks her fingers again.

I'm back in the pirate museum. I'm ten years old. And I'm angry. So angry with my dad and mum for bringing me to Little Sickle. So angry that the pirate museum, the one thing I thought might sustain me through the week, is stupid and boring. How can a museum make pirates boring! It's a crime! Nugget is saying something, but I can't hear her through the whine of my bitterness. I want to break something, smash something. I want to punish the museum. The cabinets are old; the locks barely work. I slide open a glass door and stare at the death mask of the Shark of the Straits. Resting on his eyes are white, scrimshaw coins. An eye enclosed inside another eye is carved at the centre of each. Arabic characters run around the circumference. I grab the coins and hold them tight in my fist. Slide the cabinet door closed. I start to think about what I might do with them and then I realise that Nugget is missing. I hear the screech of brakes and I'm running...

My consciousness returns to the here and now. Tears are dribbling down my cheeks. I turn away from her and run, hard and fast, running from *her*, running from the *past*, running from *everything*.

I'm so sorry Nugget, if I could make it me that was dead I would.

I hear Eloise's footsteps, steady in their pursuit. I have no idea where I am running to I just need to run, to escape this madness. I don't want to be here and I don't want to be back there.

Eloise's steps sound closer. The passageway curves to the left. I glance over my shoulder to see just how close she is at the wrong moment and... bang... white light and pain as I slam into a wooden door. I drop my phone. Glass shatters. Its beam lights the ceiling with spiders' web patterns. There's blood on my fingers when I touch my temple. Footsteps speed towards me.

The door is bolted top and bottom. I wrestle the bolts free from rusty moorings and push against the door. It doesn't move.

"Don't open that," shouts Eloise, the speed of her approach increasing.

"Open," I say through gritted teeth, smashing all my weight into the door.

With a squeal of protesting hinges the door swings open. My momentum carries me forward, through the door, off the crumbling remnants of narrow steps clinging to the cliff face, and out into the fog that swirls in excited eddies above waves smashing into the rocks far below.

Chapter 6
"No more running."

I grasp the door's metal handle in both hands, legs cycling in the air, tendrils of fog wrapping themselves around me like eels. I look down between my feet. All I see is more fog, but I can hear violent waves smashing into rocks. Their spray rises through the air. Swinging my body forward, I try to catch my feet onto what's left of the steps. My toes reach them, but come away in a shower of pebbles. The door tilts downwards as its hinges drag free of the wall under my weight. My fingers are slipping from the handle. A gust of wind sets the door shuddering.

"God's eyes, I tried to warn you," says Eloise skidding to a halt in the open doorway.

The door judders again, sliding further free from the wall. Dust and pebbles skitter over the cliff, disappearing into the fog.

"Help me. Please," I say. "Hold out your hand."

"I can't," she says, slapping a palm against the wall.

"Please, I'll do whatever you want too."

She shakes her head. Her voice is desperate. "I'm a deathling. If I touch you, you'll die. That's what we do, we take the souls from the living at the point of death."

I yell as the door begins its final parting from the wall. My left hand slips free of the handle. I'm dangling one-handed.

"Don't you dare let go," yells Eloise. "I need you alive."

I know I can't hang on anymore. I don't have the strength. This is it. I'm going to die. Fate has brought me back to the place where I betrayed my sister. It's my fault she died, now it's my turn.

"Grab the rope."

I look up at Eloise. She's untied her ponytail. Her long, curly hair blows around her face in the wind. She's holding onto the door frame with her left hand and leaning out, casting the rope that had secured her hair towards me with her right hand.

"Grab it," she commands. "I've hauled treasure sacks heavier than you."

The door is sliding further out of the wall. There's no time for hesitation. I swing my legs back, then forward, reaching for the rope with my free hand. The motion is too much for the door, it pulls free from the wall in a shower of dust and tumbles down, smashing into pieces on the cliff face.

Dangling from the slender rope in Eloise's hand, I swing into the cliff face, smacking body and face hard against the rock. I look up, blinking away dust, trying to focus. Eloise's face is set with determination as she braces a foot against the door frame and hauls me up. Within seconds, I'm lying panting and shaking on the passageway's floor.

"No more running," she says.

I can't speak. I'm still catching my breath. Still trying to believe I'm alive.

"You have the scrimshaw coins. And they're here, in Little Sickle. I can feel their power. That's why you can see me. That's why the rest of the crew is breaking through too."

"I don't know where they are?" I say. "Click your fingers, make me remember."

She shakes her head "This memory is buried deep, under too much pain. It has something to do with your sister. Dig it out yourself."

I sit up, leaning against the wall. The memories she'd pulled to the surface had been as raw as fresh wounds. I have no stomach to dig deeper into that pit of pain and shame. "I can't."

"You'll find a way if you want to help your sister."

She has my attention. "What?"

"Nugget is with us now. When she died, she wanted to cross over, but we knew she'd be useful to us, so we made her a deathling, just like me," says Eloise.

"She's nothing to do with this." Anger forces me to my feet. "You leave her out of this."

"Find the scrimshaw coins before the ball tomorrow night. Take them to the village church and then break them. Set my father free. You do this and we will help your sister find peace and pass on into the light. You have my word."

"Let her go now."

She shakes her head.

"Why must it be before the ball? What are you going to do?" I say.

"Concern yourself with your sister and nothing else. You have little time," she says, and the passageway is empty.

"What are you going to do?" I shout.

Run Tom. Her voice whispers in my ear. *Time is running out.*

I do as she says, running through the maze, turning at her whispered directions, climbing back towards the hotel. I'm sweating, panting, oblivious to the blood that has dried on the side of my face. My feet clatter against floorboards. Wood panels above and beside me. I'm nearly there. Another door.

The latch is at the right side, she whispers.

I fumble for it. Press it down. Hear the deep clunk. I lean forward with all the strength I can muster and tumble into the hotel.

It isn't the library.

My dad sits behind a table crowded with several piles of his new book. In front of him sit two dozen journalists, all staring open-mouthed at the unexpected arrival of this famous author's battered and bloody son.

~

"Let's all just calm down," says Dad.

After a visit to the local doctor to get the wound on my temple checked, we're back in his suite; him, Melloney, me and India. Fog presses against the windows permitting only grubby light through its swirls. I need the adults out of here quickly, to be alone with India; I need the Ouija board.

Melloney switches on a lamp. The bulb flickers into life. It doesn't have much effect on the gloom. "I am calm. I am always calm," she says. She's not lying.

"Me too," says India peering over her sunglasses.

"Let's put this into perspective. Tom had a bit of an accident, but he's fine," says Dad. "My press conference was over anyway and some of the journalists thought Tom crashing into the room through a secret door was part of the pirate theme."

"His face was covered in blood," says Melloney. "Did they think that was part of the theme too."

"I'm fine," I say.

Dad stares at me. "It was one of the blokes from the events company who showed you the tunnels, right?"

I nod. The less I say, the less chance I'll trip myself up. My story is that one of the Beards showed me the secret passages. We got split up. I got spooked. I tripped and banged my head. Finally, I found a way back out of the tunnels, landing in Dad's press conference.

"What was his name, I'm going to report him."

"You should sue the company," says Melloney. She's always talking about suing people. I think she'd sue me for being an inconvenient stepson if the law permitted it.

"One step at a time," says Dad. "What was his name, Tom?"

I plaster an imitation of deep thought into my face.

"Are you in pain," says Melloney.

"What?" I say.

"Your face, it looks like you're in pain."

I shake my head. "I'm fine. Just trying to remember. I think it's the bang on my head."

"Oh, I see," she says, obviously seeing straight through my lies.

"I think it was Clive... no, wait, Carl. Clive or Carl, something like that. He had tattoos and a beard."

"They all had tattoos and beards," says Dad.

"Oh, I didn't notice," I say.

Dad looks at his watch. "Look, we have to be downstairs in an hour to welcome guests to the screening. I need to shower and get my tux on. This all needs to wait. Tom, you're with me and Melloney." He kneels down in front of India. "India, honey, after your nightmares your mum doesn't think it's a good thing for you to watch the film. It might be too scary. You don't want anymore nightmares do you?"

India snorts out a laugh. "Your books aren't scary."

"Well ... they are a bit scary, aren't they," says Dad looking at me for reassurance.

I nod supportively, waiting for my moment to strike.

"We're getting Jenny, the girl from the front desk to stay with you, okay?" He says.

"No," India says. "She's a Barbie."

"What?" Dad looks up at Melloney, his face scrunched by confusion.

"Indy has issues with girls with long blonde hair," says Melloney.

"What issues?" says Dad.

"I don't like them," says India. "Barbies are evil."

Dad returns a helpless stare to Melloney. His expression reveals a profound wish that children had never been invented.

My moment has come. "I'll stay with India. The doctor said I should avoid looking at screens for too long for a couple of days."

Dad looks crestfallen. "But, don't you want to see the film?"

"Yes, of course, but I don't want to have a fit or something and embarrass you again."

"I want Tom to stay with me," says India. "Even he's better than a Barbie."

"Absolutely, not," says Melloney.

Dad and Melloney lock gazes. Not a word is spoken, but I can almost see the messages flying back and forth between them. It's like something from a sci-fi film.

M: Your son nearly killed himself. He can't be trusted.

D: It wasn't his fault and he certainly didn't nearly kill himself.

M: I don't trust him.

D: I do.

M: What about... when you were here before?

D: Do not dare bring that up... it wasn't his fault.

M: I'm just saying...

D: Well, don't! We're a family. We have to trust each other!

They hold the stare, laser eyes pushing beams of energy back and forth in a battle of wills. Surprisingly, it's Melloney that blinks first, breaking the adult mind-meld. She shifts her laser stare to me. "Promise me you'll look after Indy."

"I promise," I say.

"And that you'll stay in this room all night. No men with beards and tattoos. No secret passageways. No fog. No nothing. This room is your kingdom, everything else is the forbidden realm. Do you swear?"

"Scouts' honour."

"You're not in the scouts," snorts India.

Chapter 7

"Are there any spirits here?"

"Please, can we go now, Mel," says Dad, glancing at his watch. "They're waiting for me."

"Exactly," says Melloney, tipping her head to one side as she slips an earring into her lobe. "They are waiting for you, and they will continue to wait. You're the star. Treat them mean, keep them keen."

An hour had turned into an hour and fifteen minutes, and then an hour and thirty minutes, as Melloney showers, changes into her dress, and then decides she wants to wear a different dress. Finally, she is ready.

Dad leaves the room and disappears from sight. Melloney checks herself in a mirror, smoothing the dress over her hips, baring her teeth to make sure they're free of lipstick. She pauses at the door. "Remember your promise, young man."

"Mel! Come on!" Dad's voice sounds from the corridor.

Melloney raises an amused eyebrow and closes the door behind her.

"Thank God they've gone," says India, with the world weariness of an eighty-year-old. She slips her sunglasses from a pocket and puts them on.

"Where did you hide the Ouija board?" I say.

She shrugs. "What Ouija board?"

"India, I'm not in the mood."

"Guess," she says.

"I don't have time for guessing games."

"Yes you do. Mum said you have to stay in here all night. That means there's lots of time."

"Where is it?" I growl.

"If you want to speak to your ghost girlfriend, you'll have to guess."

"India, tell me now."

India mimes zipping her lips closed. She shakes her head, setting her razor-sharp fringe swinging.

I take a deep breath and try a placatory tone, even using her nickname.

"Please, Indy."

Her fringe swings again. "No, guess, it's fun."

I drop to the floor and peer under the bed.

"Cold, she says, smiling.

I recheck all the hiding places I'd searched earlier, in this room and hers, all the time accompanied by India and her constant refrain of *cold, colder, even colder, cold as a ghost*. She's cackling with delight now. "I love this game."

The words erupt out of me as I grab the front of her t-shirt. "Tell me where the bloody Ouija board is."

Her sunglasses fall to the floor. There're tears in her eyes. "It's under your bed," she says pulling herself from my grip and wiping away a tear.

I stalk towards the door to the corridor.

"You're horrible," she says.

My rage subsides, leaving a bitter residue of guilt. "I'm sorry. But it's important, okay?"

"Not okay," she says, slamming her bedroom door behind her.

"Damn," I mutter then call out. "Indy, come out. I'm sorry."

I wait for several seconds. She ignores me and I stomp off to my room. I drop to the carpet and peer into the gloom under my bed. Murk and shadows greet me. I tug my phone from my pocket and turn on the torch app. All it reveals is dust, a 2p coin and an elastic band. No Ouija board.

"No need to grovel," says India, standing in my bedroom door with a triumphant grin on her face. She's waving the Ouija board. "Got you!"

I clamber to my feet and sit on the edge of the bed. "You got me. Now let me have it."

She shakes her head. "You need me. You can't work a Ouija board with one person, everybody knows that."

I start to protest, but realise she's right; I've watched enough horror films to know this is a fact.

"Look," she says holding up slim white objects. "I even have candles."

I look at her, past my anger, past my need, seeing her as the fragile young girl she is. Dread crawls over me. I shouldn't expose India to this. Eloise is a dangerous spirit; rest of the Shark's crew could be worse. Who knows what spirits - what deathlings - we might summon in an attempt to speak to Nugget.

"Whatever excuse you're working on to exclude me, it won't work," she says, smiling. "You need me. And if you try to stop me, I'll scream the hotel down."

~

We're sitting at the table in Dad's suite. The Ouija board sits between us. It's the size of a large chopping board and has two arcs of alphabetically listed, gothic letters running across its width. Beneath the alphabet is one word: goodbye.

The lights are off and the only illumination is the flickering halo thrown by India's candles. Even now she refuses to remove her sunglasses. The movie's swelling music and explosions rumble through the building; it wasn't built to contain high-definition audio.

"We need a... a cup thing," I say, moving my finger over the Ouija board.

"It's called a planchette," says India heading for the bathroom.

"How do you know all this stuff?"

"Google, stupid," she says returning from the bathroom with a glass tumbler. "This'll work."

I invert the glass at the centre of the Ouija board and we each place a finger on it.

"Don't push it," she says.

"Don't you push it."

She smiles. "This is fun isn't it, Tom."

The words echo like a distant, gloomy bell in my memory. Goosebumps rise over my body. Could it be that simple?

"Nugget?" I say, leaning forward. "Is that you?

India shakes her head. "No! We haven't started".

"Oh, it's just..."

"Shut up," she says and clears her throat with a cough. She wriggles her shoulders. Closes her eyes. "Are there any spirits here?" she intones.

The room is silent. The glass doesn't move.

"Nugget? Can you hear me?" I say.

Silence.

"Please, spirits, speak to us," she says.

Candlelight flickers. The glass doesn't move.

"Nugget, please. I need to speak to you. This was your idea."

The sound of cinematic cannons firing a broadside rattles the windows.

"This is stupid, we..." I stop speaking.

India pulls off her sunglasses with her free hand so she can clearly see the icy plume of my breath roll towards her. She closes her eyes as it presses against her face.

"Don't take your finger off the glass," she whispers.

Before I can respond, the glass is ripped from us. It flies across the room and crashes through the window leaving a ragged hole surrounded by spiders' web cracks. We jump to our feet as fog rushes through the gap, filling the room like water gushing into a breached submarine.

"We have to go, now," says India, all bravado gone, teeth chattering. The room is freezer-cold. I grasp her hand.

"Wait. Look."

At the centre of the room, fog flows around an invisible shape, its full form slowly revealing itself as the room fills.

"Is it...?" asks India.

"Nugget?" I ask the girl-shaped emptiness, surrounded by swirling fog.

Hello Tom.

Nugget's voice sounds like it's in my head, a gift for me alone, but I see India flinch; she too, has heard the voice.

I try to speak. Words desert me.

It's okay.

"No it's not. I should have taken you home. It was my fault." I can't help myself, all my guilt, buried in a shallow grave for six years, is pushing upwards like a zombie hand emerging through soil.

I chose to come with you.

I shake my head. It isn't her forgiveness I'm looking for, it's punishment. "I was older. I should have known better. I shouldn't have been so selfish. All I..."

Tom, you're being selfish now.

Her words connect like a slap.

Everybody in this hotel will die unless you stop it and you can't do that if you're feeling sorry for yourself.

Fog licks my face, curls around my legs, sinuous as a cat, mocking my sudden inarticulacy.

"What do you mean?" I say.

Tomorrow night, the Shark's crew plan to burn the hotel down when everybody is at the Grand Pirates' Ball. It's the revenge they've wanted ever since the villagers murdered them.

"There'll be hundreds of kids who have nothing to do with the village," I say.

"And my mum," adds India.

They don't care. They want revenge.

"But how can they burn the hotel, they're dead?" I say.

They're not dead, they're deathlings. They're in between life and death; the nearly dead. They've been here ever since the fire on their ship, but when you came back to Little Sickle with the scrimshaw coins, the coins that hold the Shark's soul, they've been able to push so close to the land of the living. So have I. It's like we're just below a thin, rubber skin and we can push against it, stretching it, reaching into this world. The Shark is whispering to them from the coins, telling them what to do.

"But I *saw* his daughter, Eloise?"

She's dangerous. She's drawn most of the coins' magic to herself, so she can make herself seen. And maybe do worse things, I don't know the extent of her powers. But you need to stay away from her.

"How do we stop them?"

We don't, you do. You have to leave, now, and get as far away as possible with the scrimshaw coins. Without their power and his voice whispering from inside them, the rest of the crew won't be able to harm the village.

I shake my head.

You have to go.

"I'm not going."

Why?

"If I go, you're stuck with Eloise and the rest of the pirates. You won't be able to... to..."

Die properly?

"Yes, they'll keep you as a deathling forever. Do you want that?

No, it's horrible, I want to leave. But I'm just one person, if you try and save me you're putting hundreds of people in danger. Take the coins and run.

I let go of India's hand, stepping towards Nugget's empty ghost.

"Tom, please," says India reaching for my hand.

I step away from her. Fog swirls around me and the building shakes as more cinematic explosions rise through its bones. "I don't know where the coins are. I can't take them with me because I honestly don't know where they are."

They were with you when you arrived. I felt them approaching. I could hear his voice calling out to his crew. He's so powerful. It was him whispering to Dad, putting the Demon Pirates stories into his head, encouraging him to write them down. Dad never sold a book until he came to Little Sickle. The Shark's the real author of Dad's books. And after he was successful, he whispered to Dad how great it would be to return to the village with his son. It's all about you and the scrimshaw coins. It always has been.

"There has to be another way. It can't be a choice between them or you," I say.

There isn't.

India twitches, glancing left, setting the fog swirling. She let out a mewling sound and then said: "Something's coming."

Damn, it's Eloise, I have to leave! Now! She can't know I was here. They're watching me so closely. I won't be able to speak to you again, Tom. Run, get as far away as you can. It wasn't your fault. I love you.

"India, no!" I dive forward, arms open to grab her, but her ghost shape is already filling with fog and I stumble into the sofa beyond it, setting it squealing against the floorboards.

"Nugget!" I shout.

She doesn't answer.

"Nugget!"

Behind me, India lets out a startled grunt. When I turn around, her expression is blank. All this madness has been too much for her. She's slipped into shock.

"Jesus." I look around, focusing on the room; the broken window, swirls of smoke, candles and Ouija board on the table, sofa skewed halfway across the room, step-sister having a breakdown. Thunderous applause, whoops and hollers rise through the building. The movie has finished. Dad and Melloney will come back soon. "What have I done?"

I kneel in front of India and shake her. "India! India? Are you okay?" Her face remains slack, eyes staring across the room. Oh my god, this time I've lost two sisters.

Then it spears me, a memory as clear and sharp as a crystal spike driving deep into my mind. Maybe it has taken the trauma of the last few minutes to shake it free of my consciousness, or maybe it had been slowly rising to the surface ever since I returned to Little Sickle; I know where the scrimshaw coins are.

I sprint out of Dad's room, shouting to India that I'll be back in a minute. Hand shaking, I slip my plastic key into the lock and burst inside, open the wardrobe and grab my old canvas backpack; the one Nugget decorated with faded felt-tip flowers. The memory spears me again.

I'm back outside the pirate museum all those years ago. I'm kneeling by a little body in the road. I see blood on the tarmac. The Sea Blind swirls. Tears run down my cheeks. I'm saying sorry, over and over again. The scrimshaw coins are gripped tight in my fists. I squeeze harder and they bend under the pressure, cutting into my palm. In the memory, a voice whispers in my head. Don't break the coins here, it says, and there is a wheedling fear in the voice. Take them to the church, break them in the church ... in the church. But I silence the voice. I can think of nothing but the body in the road. I don't know why I do it, maybe it's the voice whispering again, but like a robot, I open my backpack and slip the scrimshaw coins into the secret pocket in its rear lining and then forget about them.

The secret pocket is hidden by a flap of fabric and secured by a small zip. I tug the zipper open and slip two fingers inside. I feel the cold bone of the scrimshaw coins and a deep voice, the voice from my memory says: *You remembered.*

I pull the coins from the bag and lay them on a palm that prickles and itches beneath their power. The bone has yellowed and sections of the carving are clogged with fluff from the backpack, but the skill used to carve the delicate eye-within-an-eye design is undiminished.

Eloise! Says the voice in my mind. *Come quickly*!

Nugget is wrong; I remember the truth. I don't need to run away with the coins to save the village. If I break them in the church, where they were first placed on the Shark's eyes, that will release him. But, if I break them anywhere else, he will be destroyed. That is why he was so afraid when I first took them. I take coin between two fingers and bend it.

There are footsteps behind me, entering the room and Eloise says: "They belong to me."

I turn. It's India, not Eloise, standing behind me. Her face is animated again, but not by any expression that belongs there. "Mine," she says again, but in Eloise's voice.

Too late, I see the club she's holding behind her back swing at my head. I yell as my vision becomes a bright flash of light. I'm falling, hitting the wood floor, trying to blink away the light. I see the scrimshaw coins slip from my grip and roll across the boards.

"Mine," says India/Eloise bending to pick them up.

Chapter 8
"Ghost fire."

I force myself up onto my hands and knees, heading spinning. "Give them back to me."

"I don't think so." Smiling, India/Eloise shakes her head and makes for the door. "Not after we've waited so long for you to find them for us."

"They're not the real ones," I mutter, still on my hands and knees. It's the only ruse my aching mind can conjure.

India/Eloise laughs, but hesitates in the doorway. Leaning forward, her voice is rich with sarcasm. "Of course not, Tom, you carved a pair yourself."

"They're fakes. Believe me."

She comes closer. "Liar, I can feel their power."

"You're imagining it, it's just what you want to feel."

"You're pathetic. I'll take these to the church, break them and then I'll be reunited with my father. When he visits you, well see who's the fake."

Her scorn brings her close enough. I launch myself at her, ignoring that I'm slamming into my little step-sister, focusing on the monster possessing her. We crash into a wall unit, setting it wobbling and a scrimshaw bowl falls to the floor scattering shards.

When I touch her, my vision changes. I no longer see the room clearly. The edges of objects aren't defined, they bleed together in foggy wisps. For one horrible second, I remember Eloise boasting that, with their touch, deathlings took human souls at the point of death, and I think I am dying. Then, I realise that I'm not touching her, I'm touching India, and by some supernatural trick I'm seeing the world as my possessed step-sister sees it.

India/Eloise pushes back against me, her strength far beyond what should be possible for India's body, and we stumble across the room, crashing into the bed. I grab her hand, trying to prise the scrimshaw coins from her grip, but I cannot move her fingers.

"You had your chance to destroy him, now it's too late," she says.

She tries to pull away from me, her strength wild and impossible. We smash into the window. My face presses against glass and I'm looking down into the car park fronting the hotel. There are figures out there, dozens of figures shuffling towards the entrance, each one carrying a heavy burden.

"You see them?" says India/Eloise. "You see what the villagers did to them?"

It's the Shark's pirate crew and I am seeing them as they died. Bodies charred black by fire. Some with hands and arms burnt to crumbling stumps. Balls of bone, each scrimshawed with an eye-within-an-eye design, have replaced eyes melted from their sockets. Sea creatures have burrowed into their flesh. Worms' bodies waggle in cheeks. Eels poke sharp-teethed heads from mouths. The pirates drag trails of seaweed behind them.

"And you see the villagers' doom?"

Each of the pirates is struggling beneath the weight a barrel. Some hold it in two arms ahead of their body, some rest it on their heads, a hand on either side.

"Ghost oil. Tomorrow night, it will make a ghost fire to consume this place and all the traitors within it," says India/Eloise.

She yanks free of me, spinning sideways and landing on her hands and knees, scuttling towards the exit like a crab. I drag a display of decorative rigging from the wall and throw it over her. Her limbs tangle in the netting. I leap onto her back, pinning her to the floor. She writhes and bucks trying to work herself free.

"Give them to me," I say, holding her down.

She hisses in my face. I grab her clenched right hand and bang it against the floor.

"What the hell's going on!" Dad is yelling at me.

"Get off her, get off her now!" Melloney's voice.

I feel Dad's arms wrapping around my chest, trying to haul me away from India/Eloise.

"No, you don't understand, she's got the coins. Everyone will die if I don't break them," I say.

I hear the breath rush out of Dad. "Oh God, why did I bring you back here? What have I done?"

His fingers prise my grip free of India/Eloise and Melloney kneels by her daughter, pulling away the netting.

"Are you okay, baby?" She says pulling India/Eloise's head to her chest.

India/Eloise nods. "We were playing with a Ouija board he found and then he just went mad."

"Ouija board?" says Melloney, turning to me. "She's nine, what were you doing making her use a Ouija board!"

"Calm down, Mel," says Dad.

"You calm down, says Mel. "Your son was just attacking my daughter."

"I think he's possessed," says India/Eloise in a voice that only nearly sounds like India. Dad and Melloney don't notice. Unseen by the adults, India/Eloise is smiling at me as she speaks.

I wrestle against Dad's hold. "She's possessed. That's not India, that's Eloise, the Shark's daughter. Stop her or everybody will burn."

"Get India out of here and find Doctor Phillips," says Dad to Mel.

"Who?"

"He's the village doctor. He was at the premier. With any luck he'll still be in the bar."

Mel leads India/Eloise from the room. The thing that had been my step-sister glances back one more time, opening her fist so I can the scrimshaw coins sitting there. She smiles and then she's gone.

"You have to believe me Dad. I spoke to Nugget. She's still here. She's helping me to fight the Shark. He wants to take his revenge on the villagers for when they burnt him and his crew."

"Nugget is dead, son. She's not coming back. I'm sorry."

"She's a deathling. I can speak to her."

Dad is rocking me, saying hush. There are tears in his eyes. "I'm so sorry son. I shouldn't have brought you back. It was so selfish of me. I don't know what possessed me. It was stupid."

"It was the Shark, he made you come back. He told you what to write in your books. It was all part of his plan. And he made you being me back here. He wanted the coins. Don't you see. Get the coins back off Eloise, off India. Please Dad."

He isn't listening. He's trapped in the grip of his guilt as tightly as I am within his arms. I wrestle against him, demanding he lets me go, then pleading, but he won't. He keeps apologising and crying. At some point, a man in a dress shirt so tight his protruding belly threatens to pop its buttons, enters the room. He unknots his bow tie and hangs it around his neck. He's talking to Dad, then lifting my eyelids, shining a torch into them, checking my pulse and taking my temperature. He asks me some questions and I'm not quite sure how I answer. I'm exhausted. I can't understand what he's saying. My thoughts are elsewhere. I have to get free. I have to stop India/Eloise.

"I'll give him a sedative," says the man, who I now guess to be Dr Phillips. He fills a syringe with clear fluid. "I think this is a panic attack."

He injects my right bicep, swabbing the entry point with a piece of cotton wool. My body goes weak. I feel my eyes close. Dad lifts me up and lays me on the bed.

I need to explain everything to Dad, I have to make him understand, but the only word I can force between my unresponsive lips is: "Scrimshaw."

Then I sleep.

~

My sleep is untroubled by dreams. It is the sleep of the dead. When I wake, pearly, fog-filtered light is entering the room. My eyelids flicker. They're heavy. I'm seeing through a barrier of eyelashes. Dad slumps asleep in a chair by the bed. He's still wearing his white shirt and has his tuxedo jacket draped over his chest like a blanket.

The calamitous events of the previous night arrange themselves like a jigsaw puzzle forced together by an impatient toddler; pictures and words out of order, jarring, incomplete. My heart races as a memory clicks into place: India/Eloise with the scrimshaw coins in her palm. She might already have taken them to the church and released the Shark.

I sit up in bed, feeling bruises where India/Eloise had battered against me. With a grunt I swing my legs free.

"Not so quick." Dad is waking. His tuxedo tumbles to the floor as he stretches. He rubs his eyes, waves a hand towards me. "Back into bed."

If I am to have any chance of getting out of this room and stopping India/Eloise, I must play my dad like never before. I do as he asks and slide back beneath the covers.

Bristles grate beneath his palm as he rubs his face. "How're you feeling?"

"Fine. Why?" I look at him as if he has just asked the most ridiculous of questions. "And what are you doing sleeping by my bed? Are you drunk?"

"No. I'm making sure there's no repeat of your antics from last night."

I shake my head, face a picture of innocence. "Antics?"

He stares at me, lost for words. He makes to speak then stops. Rubs his face again. "Fighting with India. Yelling at us, telling us we were all going to die. Something about pirates and India being possessed."

I shake my head. "I didn't do that."

"Come on, Tom." His look is quizzical, annoyed. "Stop playing around."

This will be hard. I have to use his guilt against him. I feel terrible about it, but I have no option.

"Honestly, Dad, I have no idea what you're talking about."

"Tom, you don't just forget something like that."

I force myself upright in bed, plaster an angry expression on my face. "Are you calling me a liar?"

Dad holds up his hands. "Calm down."

"Yes or no? Are you calling me a liar? Because I have no recollection of any *antics* last night. And if something did happen, it's because of this village. I didn't want to come back here, did I?"

"Tom, please..."

"Did I?"

"No, you didn't."

"Then why did you bring me? Because it suited you..."

"... Tom..."

"... because you wanted me to be here for your big day, and I understand that, but this place messed me up and all I can think of when I'm out in the streets is: this where Nugget died, this is where I let her down, this is where I was a stupid, selfish, idiot. And so if something happened last night it's because all that was too much for me."

"Okay, okay, I hear you," he says.

I can see I've wounded him, that he's on the defensive. It's time to press home my advantage. I get out of bed and surprise him by hugging him.

"I'm so proud of you and your books. It's the coolest thing ever. It's just this place. For the rest of the day I'll stay in my room and listen to music. I won't come out until the ball. Okay?"

"I don't know. Whether you remember last night or not, it was pretty upsetting seeing you that way. And you frightened India half to death."

"Do you want me to apologise to her?" I need to know where she is.

Dad looks at his watch. "That would be good, but she's already out with Melloney. They're supervising the flower arrangements for tonight. Best for them to keep busy."

There's a knock at the door. Dad opens it and waves Doctor Phillips inside.

"How's my patient this morning?" he says.

"Good I say. I don't remember last night at all."

"Hmmm," says the doctor. "Let's check you over."

He repeats some of the physical checks from last night - blood pressure, heart rate, temperature - all the time probing me with questions about the previous evening and how I feel, going back over ground to check for inconsistencies.

"I'm sure it was a panic attack," says Doctor Phillips, finally curling up his stethoscope and slipping it into his coat pocket. "Given everything you told me about your family's first visit to this village, it's not surprising there's been a reaction."

I see Dad's face flushing red, his guilt building to a new high. He's chewing the inside of his cheek, nodding then rubbing his stubble. "I know, I know. I shouldn't have brought him here."

"Look," says Doctor Phillips, laying a consoling hand on Dad's forearm. "You weren't to know. He may have been fine. You're only here for one more day, I don't see any harm in him staying. Tom just needs to take it easy. No excitement. No exploration. Everything should be fine."

"Are you sure? I could drive him home and Melloney could fill in for me at the ball?"

Dr Phillips shakes his head, checking his watch. "No need. Right got to go. More patients to see. Seems like this Sea Blind is getting to people. I have a number of my elderly female patients getting agitated by it, reporting invisible figures moving through the fog. Here's me thinking it's only teenage girls that suffer from group hysteria." He laughs as he exits. "Take care, Tom. Nice meeting you."

Dad stares at me. I can see relief washing through him; I'm okay and he gets to go the Grand Pirates' Ball. "You stay in your room until the ball, okay? I'll be texting to check on you."

"What about Melloney?"

"I'll explain things to her."

"Okay, it's a deal."

"Promise you'll stay in your room?"

"Scouts honour," I say.

He gives me a mock punch on the shoulder. "You're not in the scouts."

When he leaves, I turn on the television and find a music channel. I turn up the volume so it's just loud enough to hear from outside. Then I hang the *Do Not Disturb* sign outside my room. I wait ten minutes and then open my bedroom window. Fog swirls around me obscuring everything over six metres away. I'm only on the first floor, on the rear side of the hotel. The riot of rope-thick ivy covering the hotel means it's an easy climb to the ground.

My phone beeps. It's Dad:

Still in your room ha ha???

I text back.

No, just climbed out the window ha ha!!!

Joker. See u later.

I disappear into the Sea Blind.

Chapter 9
"Where the devils sleep."

Even though cars were arriving and departing from the hotel - their headlights cones of brightness in the dense fog - the Sea Blind makes it easy for me to slip away unseen. I jog down the curving road to the village. Behind me, bells ring out from the cliff top church announcing the end of Sunday service.

It's still early and the streets are quiet. A few people hurry along, the Sunday papers tucked beneath an arm, scarves wrapped around their faces to protect them from the freezing fog. Other than the newsagent, the only other shops open are the little supermarket - which probably never closes - and the florist.

I tuck myself into a shadowed doorway opposite the florists, identified as *Big Bloomers* by the sign above the door. Melloney is chatting to a young woman in a parka pointing at tubs of flowers arranged in rows on the pavement. She ticks a piece of paper on a clipboard in time with each jab of the florist's finger. A white van idles at the curb ready to transport the flowers to the hotel.

India/Eloise stands apart from the scene, tapping one foot, staring up into the fog, back towards the hotel and the church. She glances in my direction and I slip deeper into shadow. She maintains the stare for a few seconds then fixes a smile on her face and says something to Melloney. Her mum shakes her head and returns her attention to the florist. India/Eloise tugs her sleeves and points across the road, an imploring look on her face.

"Okay, but be quick. And watch the road." Melloney's exasperated voice carries to me.

I watch India/Eloise check the road then skip to the supermarket. Melloney and the florist are arguing about something and with a shrug of her shoulders the florist beckons Melloney into the shop. As soon as she's out of sight, India/Eloise emerges from the supermarket and sprints up the road away from the village.

I set off in pursuit.

I can hear the gravelly pavement crunch beneath her shoes. I pump my arms, gaining on her, trying to mask the sound of my approach by running on the grass verge. As we near the top of the road, the crunch of steps disappears and is replaced by a deeper thumping. She's left the road for the wide grassy area on the cliff edge that leads to the church.

I follow her, hearing my footsteps drum below me. There are nuggets of rabbit poop everywhere and the ground sounds like it's riddled with burrows.

"Looking for these?" It's India/Eloise. I hadn't heard her stop. She holds up the scrimshaw coins, her expression feral.

"India, if you can hear me, you have to fight. Kick out Eloise."

India/Eloise laughs. The fog swallows the sound.

"India, are you coming out to help Tom?" she says, tilting her head to one side as if listening. "No answer?" She laughs again and taps a finger to her forehead. "She's locked away in here. You'll get no help from her."

I move towards her. "Give me the coins."

She takes a step backwards, shaking her head, whistling as you would for an errant dog.

"You don't have to do this. These people are innocent. None of them were even alive when your father died."

"He didn't die, he was murdered. The villagers have to pay for the crimes of their ancestors."

"What about all the kids who've come for my dad's book launch? Kids from Japan, Greece and Argentina. They're nothing to do with this."

She shrugs, whistles again. "You must break eggs to make an omelette."

I charge her and she stumbles away from me, laughing. I see the reason for her good humour emerging from the fog: pirates, lots of pirates, forming a barrier between me and India/Eloise. Up close, I can see their full horror. Skin charred black by a fire so intense it's claimed fingers, noses and entire limbs. Some of their arms are nothing but bones rattling with jewelled rings. Lipless grins reveal blackened teeth. Worms and maggots burrow into skin that leaks putrescence. A mouth widens and a moray eel peers at me baring its teeth. The pirates don't have eyes; their empty sockets have been filled with scrimshaw orbs - yellowing bone carved with an eye-within-an-eye design.

"Remember when I couldn't help you at the sea stairs? When I said I'd take your soul if I touched you? I can't do that now, I'm in India's body. But my boys can." She waved a hand at the pirates. "It's been nice knowing you, Tom. With some toughening up, you'd have made a good pirate."

I back away from the pirates, but hear steps behind me. I turn. I'm surrounded by a slowly closing circle of deathlings, rotten and crumbling, shambling towards me.

"Help!" My yell dies in the Sea Blind.

A pirate starts to sing a sea shanty. His voice is as rough as stones rolling beneath the waves. Others join in, their breath stinking of brine, seaweed and rot.

"*We'll take him down*
   To join the deep
   Amidst the kelp
   Where devils sleep.
   We'll eat our fill
   Oh, when he's dead

Of bones that crack
And blood that's red."

I spin around looking for a break in the circle. There's none. The volume of the sea shanty rises. Arms reach for me. Hands flex fingers bloated thick as starfish arms; nails that have grown to claws. Their scrimshaw eyes roll in their sockets, unfixed and unfocused. I find the middle of the closing circle, making myself smaller, thoughts spinning in a useless churn. There's no way out. I wrap myself foetal-tight on the ground, oblivious to the wet earth. I think: Nugget, I will see you soon.

I can sense the pirates above me, reaching down. The crushing weight of their combined presence. The sea shanty pounds me like waves.

"We'll take his soul
A shrivelled thing
To Neptune's halls
To meet our King.
And there he'll learn
The truth of death
The truth of the lies
That's 'ner been said."

"Touch him!" It's India/Eloise. "I command you in my father's name to touch him. Now!"

I dare a glance upwards between my arms. The deathling pirates are above me, wreathed in fog, blocking the light. Their cluster of arms undulates like an anemone, straining to reach me, but all fingers stop short of my body.

"Do it! Touch him!" India /Eloise's voice is shrill with frustration.

Slowly, I raise a hand towards a pirate. His hands withdraw from mine, keeping the same distance. There's so much effort in his rotten face as he strives to reach me that a sliver of skin peels away to reveal a bed of writing maggots below.

Laughing, I stand up. The pirates fall back from me in a wave, teeth clacking in confusion and frustration.

"They can't touch me," I say to India/Eloise. "They can't touch me!"

She's already backing away. "The scrimshaw coins. You've taken some of their power. But that won't save you when they're broken."

She spins and sprints into the fog. I hesitate for a few seconds, still intimidated by the wall of deathlings, then I launch myself forward, parting the pirates like rotten curtains.

I can just see India/Eloise ahead of me in the fog. I lengthen my stride, throwing all my strength into the pursuit, listening to the drumming of the cliff top beneath me. I'm going to catch her. Her body maybe be powered by Eloise's supernatural strength, but it's still the body of a girl. India/Eloise glances over her shoulder and veers left. I follow her, closing in. Suddenly, I realise what her destination is.

"No! Stop. Eloise, stop!"

She doesn't stop. Instead she redoubles her efforts. I can't catch her in time.

"Stay where you are," says India/Eloise, skidding to a halt, turning to face me. Her breath comes in gasps, but she's smiling.

I stop, five metres away from her. She's balanced on the lip of the cliff, a wall of churning fog behind her. Below, waves boom against the rocks, heaving in and out, throwing spray high into the air.

"If you come closer, I step off the cliff," she says. "You lost a sister once before. Do you want to lose another one?"

"You wouldn't," I say.

She shuffles back a fraction and lifts a leg over the precipice. "I would."

"You'd lose the scrimshaw coins. How would you bring your father back?"

India/Eloise pats her jeans' pocket. "The coins are safe in here. If I step off, India will hit the rocks and die. I won't. I'll just find another body, climb down and get the coins."

"I don't believe you," I say.

"Okay," says India/Eloise and jumps off the cliff.

"India!" I yell, leaping forward, arm outstretched to grab her. I'm too late. She disappears from view. "No!"

How can this happen again? Oh, please God, make this a nightmare. I scrabble forward to peer down into the fog.

"Last chance," says India/Eloise. She's standing on a shelf of rock half a metre wide, the top of her head level with the lip of the cliff. "If you don't back away from me now, I jump, she dies. Understand?"

I nod at her, clambering back to my feet and striding backwards away from the edge. India/Eloise hauls herself back onto the cliff top, eyes fixed on me.

"Keep backing up into the fog and whistle so I know you're getting further away," she says.

I follow her instructions, wetting my lips and forcing out a pathetic whistle. India is alive, I haven't killed another sister. Nothing else matters at this moment.

"Whistle louder." India/Eloise is shouting now. She's moving away from me.

After a minute I no longer hear her calling out. I can't whistle anymore. My guts are churning. I stop moving and place my hands on my knees. I'm breathing heavily. Vomit gushes between my lips and I spit away stringy bile.

I nearly lost her, but she's alive. She's alive.

Wiping my lips with my sleeve, I retrace my route, moving quickly and quietly, ears strained for the sound of India/Eloise or the pirates. But, I'm alone in the fog. Not even rabbits will venture out when deathlings are abroad. I pass the point where the pirates surrounded me and push on. I know where they're going.

A grey spire reveals itself, ascending heavenward in the fog. It's the church, St. Johns. As I approach a burning sensation crawls across my flesh. I'm on fire. In an instant, my strength drains away and my head is light as mist. I collapse to the grass, my limbs twitching.

A great cheer sounds from the church. It's the sound of the deathlings welcoming their returning captain. The pirates erupt from the church into the fog. At the head of the mob stands Eloise, no longer in India's body, and a tall, powerfully built man holding an unsheathed, saw-toothed cutlass. The Shark of the Straits is free.

Chapter 10
"If you touch me, I'll take your soul."

The Shark puts an arm around Eloise's shoulders and she smiles up at him. He waves his other arm, calling out an instruction and the pirates surge away from the church like a black cloud mixing with the fog. They're heading toward the hotel.

I sprint to the church and push open its heavy door. It's gloomy inside, full of shadows. I can smell the sea and rotten flesh. I pat the wall looking for a light switch but find none.

I step forwards, footsteps echoing. What if the Shark left a deathling behind to kill me?

"India?" I whisper.

Her name bounces around the church, little more than a hiss.

I raise my voice. "India?"

"Tom?" The reply comes from close to the altar.

I find her on the floor, pressed against a pew, her knees hugged to her chest. She's shivering, her teeth chattering. When she sees me she uncurls herself and grips me in a tight hug. I squeeze her back.

"Are you okay?" I say.

"She's gone now," says India, as if this answers the question.

"Are you hurt?"

She shakes her head. I pull away from her, wriggle out of my coat and wrap her in it. Her shivering lessens.

"Thank you," she says.

Her eyes are bright even in the church's gloom. "I'm sorry," I say. "So sorry."

"You tried to save me, stupid."

"None of this would have happened if it wasn't for me."

"Stop blaming yourself, Tom. Not everything bad thing that happens around you is your fault."

My mouth moves, like a fish hauled onto the dock, as I search for words.

"We don't have time for any of this. We've not lost yet." India grips my hand. "I was in Eloise's head as much as she was in mine. I know things now. Things to hurt the Shark."

I'm still reeling from her words. She's supposed to be the child, I'm the nearly adult. But her simple sentence was like a knife cutting through the knot of guilt in my head.

"Tom, are you listening?"

"Sorry... yes..."

"Eloise was terrified you'd speak to Nugget again because she found out something important about the scrimshaw coins, something we can use against the Shark. They've hidden her somewhere."

"Where?"

"I don't know. Eloise kept hiding the memory from me. I only got a glimpse," India screws up her face in concentration. "But it has something to do with the sea. And a staircase."

I smile. "I know where she is."

~

We return to the hotel and I tell India about the secret tunnels. There's no sign of the Shark. India has a dozen missed calls and texts from Melloney on her mobile. She calls her mum, explaining that the girl in the supermarket told her that there was a cool, vintage-clothes shop in the village that sometimes opened on Sundays, that she got lost looking for it, had no signal for her mobile and had been looking for Melloney ever since... in fact, where had Melloney been all this time? On she goes.

I marvel at India's ability to turn the tables on her mum. Even so, she's forced to agree to meet Melloney in the ballroom to help finish decorating it for the Grand Pirates' Ball.

"Be careful in the tunnels," says India. "Let me know as soon as you speak to Nugget."

"You need to stay out of this now," I say. "One close call is enough. She shakes her head. "We're a team now."

"India..."

"No, Tom. You can't exclude me. I'm part of this."

I take a deep breath. "Okay. But you do what I say, okay."

"Because your plans have been so good so far?" she says.

I have to smile. "True. But I plan to improve. If you see my dad, tell him you texted me and I was listening to music in my room."

"Okay. Promise me you'll be careful.

"I promise."

In the hotel lobby, I push through swarms of overexcited kids already in their pirate fancy dress. The library is empty, roped off ahead of a private drinks reception for the village's dignitaries later. I slip inside, find the lever that opens the secret door and slip inside the passage. Barrels of ghost oil are lined up against one wall; the fuel that will turn the hotel into a funeral pyre.

I move forward, reaching back into my memory for the route Eloise took deep into the cliff. I've always been good with directions. Dad jokes that I was born with a compass in my hand and a satnav in my head. Visualising the route, I set off. Only occasionally do I use my phone's torch app to light the way.

Soon the wooden passageways give way to walls cut from stone, the ceiling high and lost in shadow. I descend a staircase. The pounding of waves rumbles through the rock like a lazy pulse. I follow my mental map, feeling a glow of satisfaction at the accuracy of my memory. I'm close to the door. I approach the last corner, a bounce in my step, and, too late, I see the faint light.

I freeze, holding my breath.

"Did you 'ear something, Lardy Linda?" The male voice comes from around the corner. It's deep and rough, the voice of a deathling.

"Nope, too many crabs in your lug holes, Monster," says a second, female voice. Of course the Shark would post guards. I should have been more careful.

"I tell you, I 'eard something," says Monster.

I back away, picking each step to avoid any noise that would betray me. Then there are voices behind me; tones raised in agitation. More deathlings. I'm trapped.

"Sounds like reinforcements on the way," says Monster. "Let's see what they want."

The lantern light bobs up and down on the wall, brightening as the deathlings approach the corner. I do the only thing I can: I climb. Bracing my legs against one wall and my arms against the other, I work my way upwards, towards the high ceiling and the shadows I pray will hide me.

As my back presses against the ceiling, I see Monster and Lardy Linda turn the corner. Monster's name is well chosen; his body is barrel shaped, and even with the damage wrought by his fiery death, he's still hugely muscled. Lardy Linda's name must have been a joke because she's thin as a twig. Her head has been burnt clean to the skull, except for a topknot of hair tied with a crimson ribbon. Her scrimshaw eyes rattle in their sockets as she walks.

I slow my breathing as the deathlings come to a stop below me. *In through the nose, out through the mouth.* My legs and arms are already trembling with the effort of holding myself in place. I adjust the position of my left arm. It's a mistake. I'd slipped my mobile into my T-shirt's pocket so I had easy access to its torch app, but now its weight making it slide forwards. I jerk my torso, halting its progress, but my new position puts even more strain on my body. Sharp pain lances along my spine.

"Hey ho," says Lardy Linda, lifting the lantern as she greets a group of three more deathlings. "What do you lot want, Gupta?"

"That kid was seen in the hotel but he's disappeared. The Shark thinks he might try and find his sister." The new group's spokesman is a pirate wearing a turban made of seaweed.

"That's why we're here, to make sure he don't get to see her," says Monster.

Gupta looks at Monster then, adjusting his turban, looks back at Lardy Linda. "I'll talk to the brains."

"Cheeky Turk," says Monster.

"I'm a Sikh!" says Gupta stamping a foot. A cloud of soot shoots out the top of his boot. "We've known each other for two hundred and thirty years, why can't you remember that."

Monster shrugs. "Ain't English, is it?"

"Save me," says Gupta, shaking his head.

A square of green light appears on my chest. It's my mobile. Thank God I set the phone to silent, and the screen is facing my chest. Even so, if they look up now, I'm done for. I twist my head towards the sliver of visible screen. It's Dad calling.

"Stop bickering," says Lardy Linda. "What's the score?"

"The kid isn't here, but he maybe somewhere behind us, in the tunnels. The Shark wants us all to spread out, to search every corridor to make sure he isn't hiding," says Gupta.

"And leave the door unguarded?" says Monster.

My phone stops ringing, but this is the least of my problems. Pain wracks my body. My arms and legs are wobbling like the limbs of a new born giraffe. I can't hold myself in this position for much longer. I'm going fall down right on top of this little deathling dispute.

"You don't have to stand next to something to guard it," says Gupta. "If we spread out, in an organised formation, we'll cover all the tunnels, there'll be no way past us. Okay? Let's go."

Monster looks at Lardy Linda.

"Do as he says you great lump," she says.

With a harrumph, the giant deathling sets off down the corridor followed by the others. Muttering, Gupta brings up the rear. A spasm seizes my right arm. I hold myself in position, but my chest dips and my phone slips from my pocket, tumbling down and disappearing into Gupta's seaweed turban. He halts, grunting and reaches up to rummage through thick, green strands. His hand comes out holding a crab, its legs bicycling.

"I told you not to jump around," he says, and pops the crab into his mouth crunching it as he disappears down the passage. I see his seaweed-turban light up at it centre as my dad tries to call me again. I'm racing time now. Because I haven't answered, he'll head back to the room to check I'm still where I promised to be.

As soon as they are out of sight, and I can no longer hear their footsteps, I collapse to the floor, breath rushing from my body in a *whumph*! My arms and legs quiver and sweat runs down my face. I rest for a minute and then force myself back up. My leg muscles ache like I've run a marathon.

Feeling my way through the darkness, I arrive at a new door baring the way to the sea stairs. A bright rectangle of light outlines it. I can smell salty air.

"Nugget, are you there?"

"Tom"! Her voice rings with happiness and surprise.

"Go down a few steps, away from the door, I'm going to open it."

"Okay."

I listen to her descend and then slide back two new bolts. Wind sucks the door from my hands and sets it banging against rock. Nugget stands three steps down, pressed against the cliff, on tiptoes. The crumbling step she balances on is only a slender ledge. Below her, waves thunder into the cliffs and spray rises heavenwards in great clouds before falling back and being replaced by the next assault.

"Come on!" I shout above the noise.

She reaches up and hauls herself into the corridor, collapsing onto the floor. I slam the door closed behind her, and drop to the ground.

"Thank you," she says, sitting on her heels and smiling at me.

There she is, my little sister, lit by the pearly glow forcing its way around the door. Her golden hair falls in a riot around and across her face.

"It was my pleasure, Megan," I say, the old game of gently mocking her real name coming naturally.

"Don't call me that," she says sweeping hair from her face to reveal her mock frown.

I think my heart might break. Listening to her speak through India, was one thing, but seeing her, seeing her as she was, is almost too much to take. She's my little sister, but she's dead. Pale skinned and otherworldly. As she moves her hair away from her face, I can see the terrible wound on her temple that killed her. My heart clenches and I reach out to hug her.

"No!" She shouts, shuffling away from me. "If you touch me, I'll take your soul. You'll die."

"I'm sorry," I say. "I forgot. It's just..."

She sees the direction of my gaze and covers the wound with her hair.

"It's what I am, for now," she says.

I swallow, trying to find an order for the words I need to say. "I wish I'd never taken you to the museum that night. I know it was stupid."

"Not now. We don't have time," she says, her voice low.

"Yes, now. I don't know whether I'll ever have the chance to speak to you again. Anything could happen tonight. I need you to know how much I love you and wish - every day I wish - that I hadn't dragged you to the pirate museum."

"The car wasn't your fault. I never blamed you. I wanted to come with you. You couldn't have stopped me if you tried. You were my big brother, and I thought you were the coolest person in the world. I still do."

I'm silent for seconds, searching for the right thing to say. All I can come up with, is: "I wish I could hug you. I wish I could make this right."

"You can make it right," she says, and her voice is urgent with excitement. "The Shark's free, but the scrimshaw coins still have their power. Now they're broken they have even more power. Enough to hold the Shark and his entire crew within them."

Adrenaline lifts me from exhaustion. "How?"

"There's a ship's log in the museum. It's the log of The Dragon Maiden, the Shark's ship. There's a page in it which every member of crew signed in blood. The Shark made them. If you place the four halves of the scrimshaw coins on that page, you'll trap the souls of every pirate named there and save everybody in the hotel. And I won't be a deathling anymore. But you only have until eight o'clock. That's when he's going to light the ghost oil."

"I can do that," I say, standing. "Just tell me where the coins are and I'll get them."

"They're at the bottom of a well," she says.

Chapter 11

"You're my hero."

I make it back to the hotel, evading the deathling pirates encircling it with Nugget's help. I sprint up stairs to my room. Seconds after I collapse onto the bed, there's a knock at the door.

"Tom, you in there?" It's Dad.

I almost laugh out loud with relief. Instead, I open the door feigning a yawn. He steps inside looking at the music video playing on television then casting a suspicious gaze around the room. Invisible to him, his daughter watches from beside the windows.

"I called and texted, why didn't you answer?" he says.

The absurd image of Gupta's seaweed turban lit a glowing green by the ringing phone almost makes me laugh. "I turned it to silent so I could have a nap. It was a long night."

"Right," he says, still scanning the room.

"You can check under the bed," I say.

"You had nothing to do with Indy going missing this morning, did you?"

I screw my face into an expression of hurt. "I was here all morning."

He stares at me for a few more seconds then sighs. His gaze slips to the windows and the blank view of swirling fog they offer. He sighs again and shakes his head. "Bloody Sea Blind."

"It'll be okay," I say. "Most people are here already."

"I know, I know. Melloney keeps telling me it provides atmosphere. Even though she knows what happened here, the Sea Blind doesn't mean the same thing to her it does to us. She doesn't have the same memories. Do you understand what I mean, Tom?"

I nod.

He turns to face me. He's put on his serious face. "I know sometimes I can be a little... how can I say this... self-focused. But I thought bringing you back to Little Sickle might help. A terrible thing happened here, but whenever I've come back to research, I've always felt close to Nugget. It's odd, isn't it? This place should only hold bad memories, but sometimes when I'm here, I feel like she's standing right next to me. My little girl with all her crazy golden hair. I half expect her to ask question after question just like she always did." He laughs, but it is a sad sound; regret and longing mixed with enduring love and fond memories.

Across the room, Nugget is crying bloody tears. "I love you, daddy," she says and covers her face with her hands

"Tom, I'm sorry, I didn't mean to upset you. Are you okay?" he says.

"What do you mean?" The words feel tight in my throat.

"You're crying," says Dad.

Then I'm hugging him and he's holding me tight. "I love you, son. You know that don't you?"

I nod against his chest. He sniffs my head.

"Why do you smell of the sea?" he says, suspicion re-entering his voice.

"I think the smell's in your nostrils, not on my head," I say pulling away from him and wiping my eyes.

There's a knock at the door and I offer thanks for the diversion. It's India, wearing sunglasses. It must have taken her a while to escape from Melloney.

"Hi Indy," says Dad. "How's your mum getting on with the decorations?"

"I think she could do with your help. She's doing that thing where she's super cool on the outside, but the killer ice-maiden inside. And she's talking about suing the events company for hurting Tom again."

"Oh, Jesus," says Dad, heading for the door. He stops and points at me and then India. "You kids need to be in your pirate costumes by five-thirty. The ball starts at six. I don't want you being fashionably late. Okay?"

"Okay," India and I chorus.

He leaves and I can hear him running down the corridor.

"Is Nugget here?" says India.

I nod. "By the window."

"Hi Nugget," says India waving at the empty space.

Nugget waves back. She's stopped crying now.

"She says hi back," I say to India.

India takes off her sunglasses. "Tell me what happened."

So I do. I tell her about the tunnels and the pirates. About suspending myself above the deathling argument. I tell her about rescuing Nugget. I tell her that the scrimshaw coins are now powerful enough to capture all the pirates. And I tell her the coins are at the bottom of a dry well close to the church where Eloise tossed them after freeing the Shark. And I tell her we have until eight o'clock to stop their plan.

"So what do we do?" she says.

"I go down the well," I say, shrugging. "There's no option."

India looks across to where I told her Nugget was standing and shakes her head. "Duh! Boys." She reaches up and taps my forehead. "Try thinking. You big man, me little girl. We find rope, you lower me down, I get the coins, you pull me up and we save the world. Easy."

I shake my head. "It's too dangerous for you."

"You just told me a story which ended with you barely being able to walk. How are you going climb in and out of a well?" she says and puts her hands on her hips.

"I can do it," I say.

India glances across the room again. "Tell him I'm right, Nugget."

"She's right," said Nugget. "And there's rope in the hotel's maintenance garage."

"She agreed with me, didn't she?" says India. "Go on, own up, she agreed with me."

And I smile; my sisters are ganging up on me.

"Okay, let's do it," I say.

~

We agree that we'll wait until it's dark to try for the coins. Even though the Sea Blind still blankets the town, it's now buzzing with tourists here for the Grand Pirates' Ball and locals caught up in the festivities. If we're found climbing down into the well, we could lose our only chance to stop the Shark.

In the meantime, India and I put on our fancy dress outfits. I'm a pirate captain, complete with a frilly shirt, long coat, a tricorn hat, stripy trousers and boots. India's outfit was made by Melloney and she moans and groans as she wriggles into the dress with its sparkly, layered skirts.

"What're you supposed to be?" I say, perplexed.

"A pirate princess," she says, shaking her head as she looks at herself in the mirror.

"Princess I'm getting. Where's the pirate element?" I say.

India holds up an eye-patch and we both laugh.

Our plan is to go down to the ballroom at six, as if everything is normal and then, as the waves of pirate kids arrive, slip away.

"Six o'clock," I say. "Let's go."

We descend the stairs into a cacophony of costumed kids and parents. The hotel lobby and all the lounges off it are crammed with scurvy sea dogs, dashing sea captains, peg-legs, dozens of demon pirates and even a few zombie ones. Dad waves to us above the sea of heads, beckoning us over as kids thrust copies of his book at him to sign.

"Ah, Tom lad, there you are captain?" he says in his terrible west country pirate accent, when we finally make it through the crush.

"This is bonkers," I say, raising my voice to a shout.

"But great." He shouts back, his eyes are gleaming with delight as he surveys the baying hoard of wannabe corsairs. He looks down at India, his smile sliding into a confused frown. "Nice costume, India. Are you a... a..."

"She's a pirate princess," shouts Melloney, squeezing through the crush and slipping a hand around his waist. She's wearing a cool outfit that makes her look like a cross between a pirate and a ninja.

"Mum, how come you get to wear a kickass outfit and I have to be Miss My Little Pirate Pony," says India.

Melloney ignores her question as she switches her gaze between our faces. "No disappearing tonight. Is that understood?"

We nod.

"I didn't hear you?" she says cupping a hand behind one ear.

"No disappearing," I say.

"We heard you," says India.

"Good. Now Peter..." She turns to find Dad already forging his way through the crowd to meet somebody, his arm raised, a big smile on his face. "Peter, wait for me."

She sets off through the crowd after him, then glances back at us. "Remember what I said."

We nod. When she's out of sight, we slip out a door into the night. Nugget is waiting for us. She waves an arm. "Come on."

"Have you seen any pirates?" I ask.

"They're everywhere," she says.

The hotel's maintenance garage is stuffed with folding beds, spare taps, plugs, extensions cables, shrink-wrapped pictures never mounted on walls, and boxes containing every variation of screw and nail ever invented. In a corner at the back of the room we find the rope.

"It's a bit thin and worn," I say, sliding it through my hands.

"I don't weight much," says India.

"And I don't know where we can find any more?" says Nugget.

We creep out of the garage and then, leaving the hotel's grounds, set out towards the church. I strain my hearing for any sign of the pirates. If possible, the Sea Blind has become even denser. I can't see further than three metres in front of me. Our only chance of advance warning will be sound, but that's being made harder by the distant thump of music from the hotel.

"This way," says Nugget, curving left past the dark shadow of the church. "The well is over there." She points dead ahead.

"Why is there a well all on its own?" I ask.

"There used to be house there too. The Shark burnt it down to get rid of the tenant but he kept the well. It's dry now."

"There's somebody up ahead," India whispers.

We stop and listen. Sure enough, we hear deathlings laughing and joking.

"Damn," I say. "We have to distract them."

"I'll do it," says Nugget.

"No way," I say.

"What did she say," asks India, but I ignore her.

"It's too dangerous."

"It's dangerous for all of us. Let me do this, please. You and India get the coins; I'll keep the pirates busy. I'm quicker than them and I'm superb at hiding."

"Tom?" says India.

I tell her Nugget's plan.

"It guess it makes sense. If you lead them away, Nugget and I can't communicate. I'd be the decoy, but I can't see the deathlings. It wouldn't take much for them to catch me."

"I know, I know," I say.

"What's the time?" asks Nugget.

I look at my watch. "Seven o'clock."

"We don't have time to debate this. It has to be this way," says Nugget.

I stare at Nugget, my little, golden sister, drinking in her face. "If I trap Eloise in the coins, I'll lose my ability to see deathlings won't I?"

She nods.

"I'll never see you again?"

"If you trap them, I don't have to be a deathling anymore. I can move on, to wherever we go next. I'll see you there... but not for a long time. Then you can tell me all about your life and adventures." She smiles, but this doesn't stop bloody tears running down her cheeks. "Bye Tom."

With this she dashes away into the fog. When she's well clear of us, she shouts at the pirates. "Hey, bonfire face! Over here!"

I see figures moving through the fog; two, three, four, five setting off in pursuit of Nugget. Above one of them a green light flashes; it's Gupta. My phone's ringing.

"Let's go," I say.

The well is twenty metres further on and unguarded. I unwind the coil of rope.

"Tom, we have a problem," says India.

I peer down into the well. It's sealed by a metal grill. "We have to drag it off," I say and continue to uncoil the rope. Halfway down its length is a badly frayed section. I ignore this - hoping that by doing so I can magic it away - then tie one end of the rope onto the metal grill. Luckily, it isn't bolted into place, just held down by its weight.

"Grab hold behind me," I say to India, and like a mini tug-o-war team, we lean back and pull. It doesn't move.

"It's too heavy," said India, through gritted teeth.

"Harder," I say.

Metal grates against concrete and the grill jerks up a hand's width.

"Come on, it's moving." I'm almost shouting there's so much adrenalin running through me.

"Aaaaghh!" India yells as she puts all her effort into pulling. Inspired by her effort, I find more energy and the grill swings up and over the lip of the well landing on the grass with a thud.

We high-five and move to the well. I tie the rope around India's waist. "You sure you want to do this?"

"Yep," she says tight-lipped.

"You got a torch app on your phone?"

She nods, flips on the light and clambers up onto the edge of the well. "I'm ready." Her smile is tight with fear. I lean forward and give her a kiss on the cheek.

"You're my hero," I say.

"I know," she says nodding with false bravado.

I lower her a couple of feet at a time.

"All okay?" I call out.

"Yep. Just smells bad." Her voice echoes.

My palms are already red and burning, but I ignore the sensation, concentrating on making India's descent as smooth as possible. The frayed section of rope passes through my hands and then over the lip of the well.

"Can you see the bottom yet?" I call out.

"Not yet." Her voice sounds distant.

"Okay. Just yell out when you're..."

The rope snaps and I'm tumbling backwards onto the grass. Winded, I lurch back to my feet.

"India?" I run to the well and I peer down into darkness. "India, can you hear me?"

There's no reply.

Chapter 12
"Keep looking."

"India? India! If you can't talk, turn on your phone. Hold it up so I can see the light." I lean dangerously far over the well's opening.

Still there's no response.

"India!"

Nothing.

I'll have to climb down and rescue her. I jump from the well, looking for something to secure the rope to, but there's nothing but the well itself, so I wind it around the base and tie it as securely as I can.

"That hurt." The words float up from the well.

I lean into the opening again. "India, are you okay? Have you broken anything?"

"Yes."

My heart sinks. Will this never end?

"My phone. Smashed the screen to bits."

"Idiot," I say, slapping the well, laughing with relief. "What about you?"

"There's no water down here, but there's mud. Lots of it. That's what stinks. So do I now. I sort of half bounced on it, half sunk into it."

"Can you move?"

There's no answer for a moment, just a sucking sound and the occasional exclamation of disgust.

"India?" I say.

"Patience."

"Any luck?"

"I have one piece. Now shut up for a minute and let me concentrate."

I measure out the length of rope I have remaining, praying it will be long enough to reach her. Scanning the fog for pirates, I add a second prayer for Nugget's safety.

"Ha! I have two and three. One to go." India's voice rises from the gloom.

I re-tie the rope around my waist and feed it into the well.

"Tom, I can't find the last piece."

A couple of minutes pass and my anxiety levels are rising again when India curses and shouts.

"Keep looking," I say.

"Like, doh."

More minutes pass. I glance at my watch. It's quarter past seven.

"Have you looked around the edge?" I ask.

She she growls her response. "Would you like to come down and look yourself!"

"I'm just trying to help."

"Well, you're not."

"It's ..."

Suddenly, India is laughing.

"What's happened?" I asked.

She's slapping the mud, her laughter coming in waves.

"India, what is it?"

"I've been crawling around in this mud for I don't know how long with the last piece of the coins stuck to my face. I must have landed on it. Let down the rope and get me out of here, I can't take this stink anymore."

I grit my teeth. "India, I've let the rope down as far as I can. Can't you see it?"

"No."

"Are you sure?"

"Yes, I'm sure."

I lean forward, lowering every last centimetre available into the well. "Feel your way around the wall," I say.

Her palms rasp against bricks. Mud farts as she circles the little space.

"I can't find it," she says. Fear is leaking into her voice.

"Try again. Work your way around. Reach as high as you can. I'll wiggle the rope."

This time she's slapping the bricks, jumping up, squelching into every landing.

"I found it," she shouts and my heart leaps. "But it's high. Too high to tie around my waist. I'll have to wind it round my wrist. I don't know if I'm strong enough to hold on all the way to the top."

"You're strong enough," I say, but think please God let her be strong enough. "Shout when you are ready."

I set myself, making sure the rope is tight around me, digging my heels into the ground.

"Ready!" Echoes up from the well.

I'm not sure where I find the reserves of energy I'm now relying on, maybe it's desperation, maybe it's energy conjured up when somebody you love is threatened; wherever it comes from, I'm a man possessed.

"You... okay?" I grunt, one foot slipping on the grass as I take another step backwards.

"Yes... can't hold on much..."

I don't register the rest of her words. My exertions are making me deaf and blind to the world. All I experience is exertion and pain with every backward step I force from myself. My hands are blistering, my back screaming. My expression is fixed, lips drawn back from my teeth, eyes screwed shut.

India screams and I am falling backwards onto the turf again. The rope has snapped. I lie back, defeated. Too tired to even cry. We've lost.

Then India screams again; with joy. "We did it."

I look up just as she dives on top of me, fixing me in a hug.

"You stink," I say.

"I don't care," she says.

She holds out a grubby palm. Resting on it are the four halves of the scrimshaw coins, their delicate eye-within-an-eye carvings clotted with mud. I hold out my hand.

"What time is it?" she says.

I check my watch. "Half past seven."

"Then let's get them." She tips the broken coins onto my hand and I close my fingers around them.

Chapter 13
"I can see a light."

We skirt past the edge of the hotel's manicured lawns, heading for the village. Music and the raucous sound of hundreds of excited young voices spills out into the night through windows opened for ventilation.

"Any messages from your mum?" I ask India.

She checks her phone's shattered screen.

"No. They're to busy being famous to care about us," she says.

I throw her to the ground, pressing her face first into the wet lawn.

"Tom!"

"Quiet. Pirates," I whisper.

They stride through the Sea Blind, across the lawns, towards the hotel from every direction.

"Are there many?" says India.

"Must be the whole crew."

"What're they doing?"

"Making sure nobody gets out alive. Come on," I say pulling her to her feet. "We're running out of time."

Keeping to the deepest shadows, we sprint down the road that curves into the village. There's nobody else on the street. They're either at the party or staying in doors to avoid the foul weather.

The Little Sickle Pirate Museum is closed and the front door looks too substantial to force open.

"There has to be a back way," I say, slipping down a narrow alleyway between the museum and the bakery next door. India follows me.

I'm right. At the rear of the building is a small courtyard stuffed with tall plastic wheelie bins and a desk chair spewing its stuffing and missing a wheel. The back door into the museum is showing its age. It has a wooden frame with frosted glass in the top half and a wooden panel in the bottom.

I grab the desk chair by its back rest and swing its base at the wood panel. The bases' wheel-less spoke crashes through the thin board. I strike it several times and then kick away the remaining fragments of wood.

Kneeling down, I peer inside. It's an office. An EXIT sign above a door bathes the room in green light. I glance back at India.

"I'm coming with you," she says before I can speak.

I shake my head.

"Yes," she says.

"I need you out here for two reasons. One: you need to let me know if anybody shows up. I don't know if I've tripped any alarms. Two: pirates could be waiting inside and you can't see them. I need to concentrate on getting to the ship's log. Believe me, this is the best way."

She holds my gaze. "Okay. But if somebody shows up, I'm coming in to get you."

"Agreed," I say, then clamber through the broken door into the office.

"Good luck," she whispers.

I leave the office and enter a short corridor. When I open the door at the opposite end, I find myself in the museum itself. Even though it's only lit by the green glow of several EXIT signs, I can see that the contents and layout have transformed since my previous visit. The tatty old cabinets are now gleaming boxes of aluminium and crystal clear glass. Touch-screen interactive displays stand alongside most exhibits. Life-sized, and life-like, mannequins dressed as pirates pose ready for action, alongside wall-mounted displays of muskets and cutlasses, daggers and plunder; all the things that I had hoped to see when I visited the museum as a kid.

Snapping out of my reverie, I move into the room, inspecting the mannequins, just to make sure none are deathlings waiting to catch me unawares. They're all waxy skinned copies; no burnt flesh, no sea creatures along for the ride. I start checking the display cabinets, searching for the ship's log, but there are so many more exhibits now; maps and artefacts, tools and clothes, paintings and scrimshawed nick-knacks, and I can't find any reference to the Shark of the Straits. When I arrive at the last exhibit, I realise why. A huge new exhibit room has been added to the museum, and it's dedicated to the Shark of the Straits.

I check my watch: quarter to eight. I rush inside, setting aside caution. At the centre of the room is a huge, very detailed model of the Shark's ship; its sails must top out at six feet. All around the room are display cases, screens and mannequins many lost in shadow due to the size of the space.

I hurry between the display cases, squinting in the green gloom and finally find the ship's log. The display case is open, one glass door slid back over the other.

"Where are you?" I say, turning to face the room. Nobody answers, nothing moves. I glance back at the ship's log. The information plate below it says:

Ship's log belonging to The Dragon Maiden, captained by Bartholomew Francis, also know as the Shark of the Straits. This page carries the signatures of his entire crew.

But the page is missing, its ragged remnants clearly visible.

"When she escaped from the sea stair it was obvious she'd tell you about the coins power." The voice is rich and deep, the words spoken precisely.

I turn to face the Shark of the Straits. He stands a few metres away from me, his tall and broad body throwing me into even deeper shadow. He's dressed in black; a long overcoat, shirt, trousers and boots. I can smell the sharpness of the sea and the cloying stench of burnt flesh. His face's skin is charred to dark, bark-like ridges around empty eye sockets. His head is burnt bald. He raises his right hand. It's as badly disfigured by fire as his face. The remnants of his fingers hold the page from the ship's log. He folds it and slips it inside his jacket.

"Give me the coins," he says, holding out a hand.

I shake my head.

"Give me the coins and I will release your sister. She can leave the deathlings and pass through the light."

I shake my head. "You don't have her."

He laughs. It's a thick sound, like boiling tar. He leans forward and smiles. His teeth are soot black and cracked by fire. I see maggots in his gums. "Experience teaches me that when foolish courage crosses swords with impatient anger, the outcome is poor for the courageous."

He sweeps his serrated cutlass from its scabbard. The air sings a high note of complaint as if it has been wounded by the blade.

"I do not tolerate having to ask for a thing a third time," says the Shark. "Now, give me the coins, boy."

"You don't have to do this."

"And why is that?"

I stare at his sword, the metal teeth running the length of its blade, and force out the words. "The people in the hotel, the people you're going to murder, they didn't betray you."

"Their ancestors did and blood must pay for its sins."

Despite the terrifying creature standing before me, I find my own anger rising, burning away my fear. "Most of the people in the hotel aren't even from here. They're here for my Dad's book. What you're doing is cowardly."

"I'm not a surgeon that takes out only the bad. I'm a butcher, and if a butcher wants bacon, he kills the pig and throws away what he doesn't need. Your father, and all those brats running around in their costumes, they're the trotters and the snout and the bones. I care not for their fate and care not to discuss this any further. Give me the coins or I will take your soul and have them anyway."

Reaching behind me, I grab the ship's log and fling it at the Shark's face, diving to the side as he swings his cutlass. It crashes into the display cabinet, bending the aluminium frame and sending shards of glass tinkling and skidding across the floor. I hear the sword whistle through the air again and continue rolling. The blade digs deep into the floorboards behind me and the Shark yanks it free scattering splinters.

I jump to my feet, looking around for something to defend myself with and pull a musket from the wall.

The Shark laughs. "You you have powder, ball and match?"

I jab the musket at him and he smashes it from my hand with three quick sweeps of his blade. I grab a plastic chair and jab it towards him. I hold onto my shield for one swing this time. The second sends it skidding across the room and crashing into the model of the ship. The Dragon Maiden wobbles on its plinth and, almost in slow motion, crashes to the floor, rigging and sails crumpling and snapping.

He slashes at me again. I lean back, losing my balance, stumbling, feet trying to adjust to keep me upright. I land on my back and breath rushes from my body. My head smacks the ground. I can't focus. I try to move but coordination escapes me. The battle is over. I tried and I failed. The Shark is a green tinged blur advancing on me. His cutlass shines as he raises it, emerald teeth waiting to bite.

"Get off me!" The Shark yells, turning on the spot, trying to wriggle free of something on his back.

I rub my eyes, vision slowly clearing and push myself to my knees. It's Nugget. She's onto the Shark's back, one arm tight around his throat, the other on his chest, hand searching the inside of his jacket. He gets a grip on her arm and peels away its choke hold.

"You'll be a deathling for eternity," he grunts as he pulls her arm clear.

But he's been concentrating on the wrong arm. Her left arm withdraws from his jacket and tosses a piece of paper onto the floor. It's the page from the ship's log; the crew's blood signatures.

"No!" The Shark tosses India across the room. She crashes into a display cabinet. Glass shatters and rains down on her. She screams, arms raised to protect her head.

Later, it would seem that the next few seconds slowed to a crawl, but I'm sure it didn't. Time can't do that, can it? It runs at one speed unless you're orbiting a black hole or some other time and space anomaly. But in my memory, I'm searching my pocket for the coins. My fingers are fumbling to grip all four pieces at once. I find them and reach out an arm towards the list of blood signatures. Above me, the Shark is bringing down his cutlass in a powerful arc. It will hack off my hand. My fingers close on the paper. The cutlass whistles towards my wrist. I can almost feel the air pushed ahead of its decent. At the last moment, I think he knows he's lost the race; he yells out a curse in a language I don't recognise.

The coins touch the paper. There's a sound like the air tearing apart, a ripping, roaring sound, and then a bang as it slams closed again. The cutlass is no more. The Shark is no more. Where he stood, the air ripples like water disturbed by a thrown stone and then slowly stills.

I lie on the floor, gasping for breath, staring at Nugget. Like breath on a mirror, she fades from view. I reach out to her, groaning at the effort, but she shakes her head.

"It's time," she says, smiling.

The smile is all I needed to see. I blow her kiss.

"I can see a light," she says, and then she's gone.

A laugh forces its way out of me. I roll onto my back letting it take hold. Tears of relief and joy and I don't know how many other emotions slide down my cheeks. Finally, they are only tears of grief. I have lost my sister, but things will be okay. She will move on to the place where we go next. And I will see her again, one day. My tears stop. I push myself up and sit cross-legged amongst the devastation.

Footsteps thunder through the museum. India rushes into the room, the look of horror on her face sliding away when she sees me. "Did we do it? Is he gone?"

I nod. I'm too tired to speak.

She looks around the room at the broken cabinets, the shards of glass, broken musket, the scuttled ship and whistles.

"We'll have to think of a great story to get out of this one," she says.

I nod again and smile.

"Come on," I say. "Let's get out of here."

My legs feel heavy as anchors as I trudge through the museum and out into the foggy night.

"Tom Simpson?"

The voice startles me. My gaze finds the figure, indistinct in the swirling fog on the opposite side of the road. It's a teenage boy. About my age and height. His expression is dark, serious. I feel India squeezing my arm as she peers past me.

"Maybe," I answer. "What do you want?"

"I want your help." He says.

Weariness moves through me like a wave. "Oh yes? Maybe another day," I turn and start to walk down the street with India at my side.

"Today, I'm afraid," he says. "They're already on the way."

I turn to face him. Suddenly, I feel very cold; as if marrow has been removed from my bones and replaced by fog. "Who are you?"

His smile is as weary as I feel. "I'm the son of Death. But most people call me Stan."

THE END

GET A FREE COMPLETE NOVEL, AWARD-WINNING SHORT STORY

& EXCLUSIVE DEATHLINGS SHORT STORY

Building a relationship with my readers is the very best thing about writing. I occasionally send newsletters with details on new releases, special offers and other bits of news relating to my books.

And if you sign up to my Reader Group, I'll send you all this free stuff:

1. A free copy of Book 1 in the Deathlings Chronicles: **All The Dead Things** (averages 4.4 out of 5 stars and RRP $3.99

1. A copy of one of my favourite short stories **Manny and the Monkeys** (a blackly comic horror story that won the **British Fantasy Society Short Story Competition**).

1. A new Deathlings Short Story – **Interview with a Deathling**. Exclusive to my mailing list – you can't get this anywhere else.

To receive the novel and two short stories, visit simonpaulwoodward.com

Enjoy this book? You can make a big difference.

Reviews are the most powerful tools in my arsenal for getting attention for my books. Much as I'd like to, I don't have the financial muscle of a New York publisher. I can't take out full-page ads in the newspapers or put posters on the subway.

(Not yet, anyway).

But I do have something much more powerful and effective than that, and it's something that those publishers would kill to get their hands on.

A committed and loyal bunch of readers.

Honest reviews of my books help bring them to the attention of other readers.

If you have enjoyed this book, I would be very grateful if you could spend just five minutes leaving a review (it can be as short as you like) on the book's Amazon page.

Thank you very much.

ABOUT THE AUTHOR

Simon Paul Woodward is the author of the **Deathlings Chronicles** series and **Dead Weapons**. He makes his online home at www.simonpaulwoodward.com. You can connect with Simon on Facebook at www.facebook.com/simonpaulwoodwardauthor and send him an e-mail at simonpaulwoodward@icloud.com if the mood strikes you.

ALSO BY SIMON PAUL WOODWARD

ALL THE DEAD THINGS: Deathlings Chronicles Book 1

A boy on the run. A dead girl leading a rebellion. Time is running out to save the world of the living.

The deathlings believe Stan is the Seer, a human destined to be their doom. They'll stop at nothing in their pursuit of him, even breaking time itself. Now Stan must find his way to the truth, before the deathlings steal his soul. If he fails, they'll destroy the balance between the worlds of the living and the dead forever.

Buy it on Amazon

ALL THE DEAD SEAS: Deathlings Chronicles Book 2

Pirates rising from the grave. A Cornish village that may not survive the night. A boy fighting to save his dead sister's soul.

Tom blames himself for his sister's death. When he returns to Little Sickle, the village where she died, he's shocked to learn that her soul is still imprisoned there. Now he has one night to face his guilt, uncover the village's wicked past and rescue her from a crew of bloodthirsty, deathling pirates. Damnation or redemption will be his by dawn.

Buy it on Amazon

DEAD WEAPONS

A young man framed for murder. Cyborg black-ops soldiers. A race to save a missing father.

Ciaran agrees to do one last job for this gangster brother. Delivering an AI-powered gun, stolen from a covert government agency, to an underworld boss. As payment, he learns that their soldier father's death was faked. When the job goes wrong, he's framed for murder and forced to flee the police, gangsters and cyborg black-ops soldiers. As his pursuers close in, Ciaran discovers a link between his father's disappearance and the covert agency. Now it's a race against time to stop their plans and save his father from a fate far worse than death.

Buy it on Amazon

DEAD WEAPONS - 2 Chapter Sample
Simon Paul Woodward

five days until he dies

BBC NEWS WEBSITE

Murder Trial Date Set for Military Vehicle Armed Robbers
    Following one of the fastest major investigations in the history of the Metropolitan Police Force, the armed gang led by Patrick Richards is set to face trial in two weeks on charges of armed robbery and murder.
    It was only a month ago the Met released shocking CCTV footage showing masked men using two flatbed trucks to block in an armour-plated military vehicle, before overwhelming its security detail. During the robbery the driver, Sergeant Wayne Chin, was shot and mortally wounded. All the gang were apprehended at the scene of the crime except for Patrick Richards who evaded capture for 48 hours. The Ministry of Defence has not released exact details of the vehicle's cargo or ......

CHAPTER 1

The ringing phone jolted Ciaran from his bed — one ring, two rings, stop. Its echo ran through him like electricity. He crept out onto the landing, body pressed against the wall. The phone sat on a little table in the hall below.

It might be a coincidence. It might not be him.

He jumped as the phone rang again: one ring, two rings, stop. His mother, Sinead, cursed as she halted her second dash for the phone and stomped back to the kitchen.

I'm going to ignore him.

But he knew he couldn't. He tiptoed downstairs and lifted the handset. His mum was in the kitchen, at the end of the corridor, washing bowls and mugs from breakfast. Flurries of snow danced beyond the window. The sky was slate grey except for a few clouds as dark as bruises.

He turned his back on her and keyed through the phone's call log. Two missed calls with the same number. He didn't recognise it, but he could guess where it was coming from and who was dialling. This was Patrick telling him he needed to talk urgently, privately. It was a code: two rings, cut off; two rings, cut off; pick up on the third ring and make sure there was bloody well nobody else around to overhear.

I'm not going to answer it.

He fumbled the phone when it rang.

"Got it," he said, pressing the receiver to his ear.

"This is a call from Her Majesty's Prison, Brixton, will you accept the call?" said a recorded voice.

The answer snagged in his chest like indigestion. The message repeated the question.

"Yes."

The line clicked. Somebody was breathing into the receiver. Behind this, voices shouted and metal slammed against metal.

"Who is it?" His mum stood in the kitchen doorway, soap suds dripping from her fingers. She wiped them on a tea towel.

"G."

"G? Who's G?"

"That's his name."

"Any other letters?"

"Who're you, the cops?"

"I'm your mother, for my sins. And today your mother's not in the mood for any of your lip. Who's G?" Her Irish accent was always more distinct when she was angry.

Ciaran sighed. He could hear Patrick's breath as he waited on the other end of the line.

"*George,* the street dancer. Sideways hats, baggy pants, self-taught suicide flips. I showed you one of his clips on YouTube.

"Don't lie to me, Ciaran."

"I'm not."

She stared at him. *They* stared at him; his mum from the kitchen doorway, his dad from the picture on the wall. His dark face, proud and handsome, smiling from beneath the peak of a marine's cap. A medal, awarded for gallantry, gleaming on his chest.

Sinead was looking at the picture too. "Your dad hated lying."

"I hated him *dying*."

Sinead blinked, searching for words.

"Hurry up, soldier, clock's ticking," said Patrick, his voice was taut. "Get her out of there."

Ciaran looked at his dad's photo then back at his mum. Took a deep breath.

"It's George, okay. Go on, talk to him." Ciaran held out the phone. "If you don't trust me."

She took a step forward, reaching for the phone, staring into his eyes. Tinny sounds escaped the receiver. They held each other's gaze. Finally, she shook her head and dropped her hand.

"You'll be the death of me," she said, hurrying back into the kitchen, thighs bumping the sink, slamming a bowl into the soapy water. Suds leapt into the air and splattered onto the floor. She cursed but didn't move to clean them. Her shoulders rose and fell, as if she was laughing, but Ciaran knew she wasn't. He opened his mouth to say something, but Patrick was in his ear.

"She gone?"

"What do you want?" said Ciaran, pressing the handset to his ear and lowering his voice.

"Did you see I got a trial date?"

"I don't care."

"Nice to speak to you too, little brother." Patrick laughed.

Ciaran didn't respond. Prison sounds filled the silence: voices raised in argument and high spirits; somebody cackles, then coughing and spitting; metal doors clanging shut, the sound echoing; keys rattling in locks; pool balls click-clacking, laughter, and heavy weights thudding onto workout mats.

"Why did you change your mobile number?" said Patrick.

"Why d'you think?"

"Don't know, that's why I'm asking. I bought you that phone so I could contact you if I ever needed to."

"I never wanted to speak to you again."

Patrick sighed, as you might at the antics of a troublesome child. "You still not got over that yet?"

Ciaran pressed the phone to his ear, squeezing the plastic rectangle until it creaked and its seams bulged. He wanted to swear at his brother, to punch him in the face. He closed his eyes, and he was momentarily somewhere else: wind tugging at him, a metal bar gonging against a metal sheet, someone screaming and screaming.

"We haven't spoken for two years, get to it. Why're you calling?" said Ciaran.

"Come with her today."

"What?"

"You heard."

Ciaran glanced over his shoulder. His mum was out of sight. He could hear crockery rattling as she stacked it into a cupboard. "Why?"

"It's visiting day. Come and visit me."

"You joking?"

"Do I sound like a comedian?"

"No, a nutter."

"I need to talk to you."

"I'm listening, tell me now."

"It has to be in person."

"Why?"

"You'll understand when I tell you."

"I'm not coming. I hate you."

Patrick sighed again. "We're brothers."

Ciaran leant forward almost hissing into the phone. "Brothers don't do what you did. I'm hanging up."

"Wait I –"

"Bye, Patrick. Don't call again."

Ciaran had pulled the phone away from his ear but he still heard Patrick's words.

"Dad's not dead."

Ciaran felt the corridor tilt. He glanced to his left and his dad's portrait smiling down at him. His *dead* dad. Blown up by a roadside bomb in Yemen.

"Liar," he said.

"It's true. I know what really happened."

The phone creaked as Ciaran squeezed it even tighter. "You're a liar!"

"Well, if you don't come, you'll never know for sure, will you, little brother? And if you say a word to mum, or anybody else, I won't tell you anything. See you later."

The dialling tone filled his ear, his skull and his thoughts were senseless vibrations. He lowered the phone to its charging cradle. When he turned around, his mum was standing in the doorway, arms crossed, her eyes dark with anger.

"How's G? Did he change his name to *Patrick* halfway through the conversation?"

"I didn't –"

"Save it, you're not coming."

She turned away, leaving Ciaran standing in the hallway beneath his dad's never changing smile.

~

She made ready to leave soon afterwards. He threatened disobedience and then pleaded for understanding, but she repulsed both tactics with silence.

Pulling on her coat, she turned to him. "Be honest with me, for once. Why today? You've never wanted to see him before."

If you don't come, you'll never know for sure will you, little brother? If you say a word to mum, or anybody else, I won't tell you anything.

"Just because," he said.

She slammed the door as she left.

He waited for a minute, paralysed by indecision, then pulled on a hoodie and jacket, grabbed his house keys and ran down the street. At the corner, four kids wearing puffa jackets over school uniforms sat astride BMX bikes their laughter dying as Ciaran approached. They were older than him, sixteen, some seventeen, but he was taller and broader than all of them.

"Give me your bike, Fish." Ciaran grabbed the handlebars.

"Leave it out." Snowflakes settled on the kid's Afro as he tried to yank the bike free of Ciaran's grip.

"I need it. Business," said Ciaran.

"What's happened to you, bruv? Why don't you hang around with us no more?"

"Why should I?"

"We were mates. Remember?"

"I don't need mates anymore. Give me the bike."

"You're having a laugh."

"Remember who my brother is?"

"Everybody knows Paddy Richards, man."

"I'm doing a job for him."

"He's inside," said a kid whose acne clustered around his roman nose like filings around a magnet.

"You think everything stops because of that? I can tell his crew you didn't help?"

Fish swung his leg over the crossbar. He glared at the other kid, raising an eyebrow. "Didn't say that, did you, Nozzle?"

Ciaran jumped on the bike and pedalled. His mum was already climbing aboard a bus. One kid shouted after him, but the wind ripped up his words.

Gusts whipped the strengthening storm into Ciaran's face, numbing his cheeks. Snowflakes stung his eyes. He cut across the park, wheels slipping and sliding on the slim white blanket covering its paths, and jumped the bike into a tangle of snarling traffic behind the bus. Cars were bumper to bumper, edging forward, engines growling, wipers dumping blades of slush at the edge of windscreens.

He wove his way between the traffic. Frustrated and suspicious glances followed him from behind condensation beaded windscreens. He retreated into his hoodie's shadows, into the darkness enveloping his thoughts.

Dad's not dead.

Liar!

I know what really happened to him.

Liar!

The static queues of traffic passed in a blur of silver, blue, black and red.

How could he say something like that? Why would he?

Minutes became tens of minutes. He was lost in spinning thoughts.

"Watch where you going, you little toe rag." A riot baton jabbed into Ciaran's stomach bringing him to a sudden, gasping halt.

A line of policemen blocked the road. They were holding batons, bulked up by layers of black riot armour, breath clouding like bulls in a field on an icy morning. Beyond them, an anti-war demonstration snaked by, with protestors waving slogan-daubed banners and placards.

STOP THE WAR!

REFUGEES ARE PEOPLE TOO!

BULLETS + BOMBS = MORE HATE!

Somebody was banging a drum. A group of girls blew hard into droning horns. A grey-haired woman chanted through a loudhailer:

"STOP THE DIRTY WAR! THE WAR WE ALL ABHOR! THE SAND IS RED WITH YEMEN'S DEAD! WE CAN'T TAKE ANYMORE!"

"I need to get through," said Ciaran.

"Go around," said the policeman, not meeting his gaze.

"But –"

"Go. Around," he repeated, glancing over his shoulder as yells filled the air.

A pushing contest between demonstrators and the line of police mutated from see-sawing to and fro into a scuffle. Officers surged towards the incident, body armour moving like insect chitin as they swung batons. Demonstrators screamed, shouted in defiance and blood splattered the dirty, snowy ground. The crowd surged backwards, people falling over as they tried to move beyond the reach of the batons.

Ciaran used the distraction to slip past the fractured police cordon into the main body of the demonstration which was hurrying away from the disturbance. All around him, people were twisting their heads to keep an eye on events behind them.

"Fascists!" a man shouted, breath rolling through the air. Ciaran expected the heckler to be a crusty with dreadlocks and rings in his nose, but it was middle aged man in an anorak carrying a toddler on his shoulders. Others joined in, hurling insults towards the police as the woman continued to shout through her loudhailer.

"STOP THE DIRTY WAR! THE WAR WE ALL ABHOR! THE SAND IS RED WITH YEMEN'S DEAD! WE CAN'T TAKE ANYMORE!"

A group of six or seven younger demonstrators with checked scarves wrapped around the lower half of their faces were weaving their way back through the crowd towards the disturbance. A lighter sparked into life and flames took hold of a cloth soaked in fuel. Six Molotov cocktails arched through the air, setting off a mixed wave of screams and cheers, before crashing into a group of riot police and spreading fiery puddles of petrol.

Police officers stumbled backwards beating at flames. One spun on the spot, screaming as the flickering tongues rising from his back spread to engulf him. A colleague sprinted to his aid, spraying a white cloud from an extinguisher.

"Take your positions!" A line of officers knelt and loaded their rubber-bullet guns.

"Aim for the ring leaders!" The officers raised their guns, sighting the length of the barrel.

"Fire!"

The guns popped and rubber cylinders cut through the crowd. Demonstrators spun and dropped to the wet ground, wheezing or unconscious. A man clasped a hand to a bloody mouth, looking at shards of teeth on his palm.

"Reload and fire!"

The crowd erupted into a seething mass of violent, uncoordinated and multi-directional panic. The police fired again. Officers waded in from every angle swinging batons. All around Ciaran, demonstrators tripped, stumbled and fell. Comrades who'd been standing shoulder to shoulder minutes before, now trampled over each other in a blind panic to escape the mayhem.

A rubber bullet whizzed over Ciaran's head and a surge of bodies smashed into his bike. He stumbled forward and fell hard on the handlebars and pedals. A knee whacked him on the temple and he lost a few seconds to swirling confusion. If it hadn't been for his bike tripping up some of those around him, he might have been trampled. Instead, the majority of the stampeding crowd stumbled around him.

As soon as the press of people had thinned enough, he bashed his way through to a side street, foot on a pedal, using the bike as a scooter, then swung his leg over the crossbar and fled the bloody maelstrom behind him.

~

Fifty minutes of lung-busting pedalling later, his face dead with cold and his trainers soaking wet, Ciaran skidded to a halt outside the prison. He had to wait another freezing ten minutes before his mum arrived. She cursed and brushed past him.

"You can't stop me." He dumped the bike and followed her.

"Oh yes I can." Sinead spun to face him. "He's going on trial for murder. Murder! You do understand what sort of man your brother is, don't you, Ciaran?"

"I don't *want* to see him, I *have* to."

"Why?"

Ciaran shrugged. "I just do."

"That's not good enough."

"If he's so bad, why do you still visit him?"

Sinead sighed, walked away, then turned back to face him.

"Because he's my son and I love him despite everything he's done. I can't help it. It's the cross I have to carry as his mother. But I love you too and I don't want you to turn out like him. It'd break what's left of my heart. And wherever your dad's looking down on us from, it'd break his heart too."

"He doesn't get a vote," said Ciaran. "He's not here."

"Ciaran ..."

"No, I'm not talking about that. Okay. If you love me, you'll let me see him, or you might lose me too."

"Now that's –"

"I have to see him."

Her eyes filled with tears and she turned away. "Have it your way."

CHAPTER 2

Sinead bent to sit at an empty table.

"Not there." The prison officer pointed to the far edge of the room. A tattoo peaked out from beneath his cuff; a woman's legs, feet in stilettos. "Over there."

Ciaran glared at the officer. The officer returned a look dripping with contempt. "Come to see where you'll end up?"

Sinead grabbed Ciaran's arm and dragged him across the room. The guard muttered, "Runs in the family," to a shorter officer standing at his side and they both laughed.

Ciaran yanked his hand free of Sinead's grip and slumped onto a chair. Its rubber feet had worn away and bare metal squealed against the hard floor as it moved beneath his weight. The prisoner sitting at the next table glared at him, shook his head and then returned his attention to his female visitor.

The visiting room was hot, with condensation frosting high windows. Ciaran wrestled free of his jacket. His body was overheating after his run-in with the riot police and cycle sprint across the city. Sweat ran down his face and back and dark rings formed around his armpits. He wrinkled his nose. The room smelt of disinfectant and sweat.

"Keep your opinions to yourself, eh, pal."

"Or what?"

The altercation was in the middle of the room. Two prisoners facing off from their respective tables. One had a narrow pock-marked face; eyes bulging, head twitching on a scrawny neck. The other was thickset, his face a slab of meat. He raised a thick arm and flicked out his fingers as if shooing away a fly.

"Oh yeah? That it?" said Pock-Marks.

"Play nicely or it's visiting time over," said a prison officer rising from his chair.

A door squeaked open and Ciaran sensed his mum tense. Patrick entered the visiting room. He was tall and powerfully built with a shaved head and thick forearms tattooed with mathematical equations; *the meaning of life* he always said.

A moan escaped his mum's lips as Patrick limped across the room. He was dragging one leg, holding his right arm tight to his body, grimacing with each step. There were bruises on his cheek and discoloured, swollen skin around his eyes.

As he came close, Patrick twitched his right hand, keeping his fingers screwed into a fist. It was a signal to Ciaran, something they used back when Ciaran used to run errands for him; he had a note to pass. Ciaran didn't acknowledge the signal and a flicker of irritation creased Patrick's face. Gritting his teeth and hugging his ribs, he lowered himself into a chair opposite Ciaran and Sinead. He blew out a breath. "Mum. Bro."

"What happened to you?" said Sinead, reaching out to touch his face.

"Slipped in the shower, didn't I, officer?" he said, turning to face the nearest guard, who ignored the comment.

"You have to report whoever did this."

"Don't work that way." Patrick sighed. "Look, I have something that somebody else wants. They sent someone to get it. But I didn't want to give it to him. So now, I look like this, and he's visiting the NHS. It's just business."

"Business?" said Sinead, failing to hide the scorn in her voice.

"Yes, business, you know how it is." Patrick's smile revealed a chipped incisor.

"No I don't and I'm not interested in your games today," said Sinead. "Why did you force Ciaran to come?"

"Nice to see you too, Mum," said Patrick laughing.

"Please, I'm begging you. Leave him alone. Haven't you done enough damage?"

"Can't a man just miss his little bro?" Patrick shifted his attention to Ciaran. "How's tricks, Bro."

Ciaran shrugged, as always struggling to keep his composure in his brother's darkly, charismatic presence.

"It's good to see you, man." Patrick leaned across to punch Ciaran on the shoulder with his right fist. Ciaran's gaze followed the fist. He tensed, making ready to grab the note and stuff it into his pocket before anybody saw it.

"Stop looking at me!"

It was Pock-Marks, screaming at the neighbouring table. He launched himself at Meat Face sending chairs and tables clattering in every direction. Prison officers surged towards the fight, yelling commands, stumbling over fallen furniture. Another brawl broke out. Raised voices filled the room. Visitors screamed. An alarm clattered into life.

Ciaran and Sinead were on their feet, backing away from the maelstrom at the centre of the room, when a surge of bodies separated them.

"Ciaran!" Sinead tried to push through a wall of tattooed muscle.

Ciaran turned to help her, but a hand gripped his shoulder.

"It's all planned." Patrick's breath brushed his ear.

A piece paper crumpled into his hand. His brother spun him around, his face pressed close as he whispered. His breath smelt of onions and cigarettes.

"There's an address on the paper, it's a garage under some arches. Don't go tonight, wait a couple of days just in case somebody's watching you. At the back of the lockup, under a tarp, you'll find a metal briefcase. When you've got it, call the number on the bottom of the paper. They'll tell you where to take it. Okay?"

"What about Dad? Tell me what you meant on the phone."

"Check the paper, Bro. Quickly." Patrick glanced around.

Ciaran opened his hand and unfolded the paper. He saw the address and telephone number. "What?"

"Other side."

He turned the paper over and found a grainy, scanned photograph; a man standing in front of a newspaper stand, a railway station's departure boards in the background.

Ciaran felt the room tilt around him. "It can't be him."

"It's him."

"It's a trick. This is an old photo."

"Look at the newspapers."

Ciaran squinted at the image. He could just make out the face on the front of the newspapers, the headline below: RIP Rubicon. It was the day the American rapper X-da-Rubicon was murdered. That was two weeks ago.

Ciaran shook his head. "Where is he?"

"Deliver the case and we'll talk again."

"Tell me now," said Ciaran grabbing the front of Patrick's prison overalls.

Patrick prised Ciaran's fingers free. "The briefcase. You get that to where it needs to go, I have my get-out-of-jail-free card, then I'll tell you everything."

"What's in it, drugs?"

"Nothing's in the case. Don't open it."

"Somebody's going to get you out of jail for an empty suitcase?"

"Something like that. Remember where I said it was?"

"At the back of the lockup, under a tarp," said Ciaran.

With a grunt, Sinead wriggled her way between two cons and Patrick moved away from Ciaran. "What's going on, Patrick? They were keeping me away from Ciaran. I know they were."

"Nothing's going on," said Patrick. "I'm just keeping him safe."

"I don't believe you." She switched her attention to Ciaran. "What did he say to you?"

Ciaran screwed the piece of paper tight in his fist. "Like he said, he was just keeping me safe."

Continue the adventure by visiting Amazon
Or www.simonpaulwoodward.com

Printed in Great Britain
by Amazon